THE CLEARING

THE CLEARING

HEATHER DAVIS

G RAPHIA

Houghton Mifflin Harcourt
Boston   New York   2010

Graphia and the Graphia logo are registered trademarks of
Houghton Mifflin Harcourt Publishing Company.

www.hmhbooks.com

Text set in Garamond MT
Book design by Susanna Vagt

Library of Congress Cataloging-in-Publication Data

Davis, Heather, 1970–
The clearing / Heather Davis.
p. cm.
Summary: Amy, a sixteen-year-old girl recovering from an abusive relationship,
moves to the country in Washington to live with her great-aunt, and there she
discovers a mysterious clearing in the woods where she meets Henry, a boy stuck
in the summer of 1944.

ISBN 978-0-547-26367-0

[1. Space and time—Fiction. 2. Interpersonal relations—Fiction. 3. Country life—
Washington (State)—Fiction. 4. Great-aunts—Fiction. 5. Schools—Fiction. 6.
Washington (State)—History—20th century—Fiction.] I. Title.

PZ7.D28845Cl 2010

[Fic]—dc22

2009032965

Manufactured in the United States of America
DOM 10 9 8 7 6 5 4 3 2 1

4500213438

Each night I wished for things to be different. I'd lie awake in the cool darkness, breathing in the smell of fabric softener on my pillowcase and listening to the sound of the late-night TV show coming from Mom and Pete's bedroom. And I wished myself far, far away.

I'd imagine a life far away from the bland, new houses in our quiet Seattle cul-de-sac. A life far away from the green, green lawn of my immaculately maintained high school. A life far away from Matt Parker and the bruises he left on my arms.

And those bruises you couldn't see.

I admit it. For the last year, I'd been a little dumb. Totally focused on Matt Parker, until the day he forgot I existed. And then all I wanted to do was vanish for real. To disappear into a mist, never to be heard from again.

Every single night that summer, I lay awake wishing my life were different. And then one day it was . . . but not in the way you probably think.

Different was my great-aunt Mae's singlewide trailer and forty acres of trees and grassy farmland.

"You sure you'll be all right here, Amy?" Mae smoothed some flyaway gray hairs under her straw hat. "It's just farmers and old folks in the valley."

Mosquitoes buzzed around us in the cooling September air,

and Katie, the German shepherd, sniffed at me uncertainly as Mae and I pulled my stuff from the bed of her rusty Ford pickup.

"'Course, Katie and I are happy to have the company," Mae added. "Even in our humble abode."

"This place is great," I said, trying to sound convincing as I glanced at the ramshackle trailer in front of us, with its sagging wooden steps and faded, salmon-shaped windsock that flapped randomly in the afternoon breeze. I'd seen Mae's home once before, when Mom and I visited Rockville when I was a little kid. The place seemed kinda run-down now, but I didn't care that much.

I'd always liked Mae. Every year she visited us at Easter, Thanksgiving, and Christmas, bringing jars of homemade jam and fresh honey from her beehives. And to me, a country life with trees as far as the eye could see and a sun-dappled garden seemed a paradise compared to what I'd left. Short of running away, it was my only option.

The fact that my mom hadn't argued with me about moving up here to this tiny town in the North Cascade Mountains had hurt a little. In some ways she was probably relieved I was going away for senior year. Pete's kids were off at college, and with me out of the picture, Mom and Pete had some alone time. Yeah, Mom had agreed with me when I told her I needed to get away. At least she understood that transferring to another high school in the city wasn't going to help when Matt and my old crowd of friends lived less than a mile away.

And so there were a couple of days of packing, and then I left with no goodbyes to anyone, except Mom and Pete, who'd driven me to meet Mae halfway between Seattle and Rockville at a rest stop on the highway. I needed to be somewhere different. Maybe I needed to be someone different, too.

Mae helped me drag my suitcases and box of books up the stairs of the mobile home, Katie trotting behind us and woofing her encouragement. The fresh country air, which smelled of rain and cut grass, disappeared behind the closed trailer door, replaced by stagnation and a damp staleness that seemed to penetrate everything inside. Mae took my coat and hung it on the peg next to hers on the rack. Then she wriggled out of her rubber boots while I checked out my new home.

At one end of the living room, a wood stove stood on a brick hearth, flanked by a new-looking tweed couch and two bookshelves overflowing with books and DVDs. Off to the left were a kitchen and eating nook, and to the right, a narrow hallway.

"It's smaller than I remembered," I said. Then, seeing Mae's face fall a little, I added, "Of course, everything seems big when you're a little kid." Sheesh, the last thing I needed was to wear out my welcome in the first ten minutes.

"That is true," Mae said. She opened the wood stove and poked around with a stick to stir the fire, then clanked the door shut. "Though I expect after the trouble you've had, it'll do you good." Mae gave me a smile that crinkled the lines around her mouth. "Be just the balm you need to heal what ails you."

I didn't know how much Mom had told her about everything, so I just said, "It'll be okay." Katie nosed my knee and I gave her a pat.

"Your room's down the hall past the bathroom, sweetie. You get settled and then meet Katie and me out by the woodpile. We've got some splitting and stacking to do for winter."

"Sure." I sighed. So that was Aunt Mae's real balm for what ailed me—manual labor. Did sweat and splinters heal a total life implosion? I doubted it.

I wheeled my suitcase down the narrow hall and opened the door with my toe. Cramped but clean, the room had a bed, desk, chair, dresser, and closet. Lilac sheets peeked out from under a white comforter on the twin bed; a hand-stitched quilt was laid across the foot.

A fresh start. A simple room in a new place where no one knew me or what I'd come from. A place to lose myself—and all that had come before.

The next morning, I woke to the sound of Mae's truck roaring off down the driveway. Sitting up in bed, I noticed my arms were sore from last night's chores. Mae did a lot of things the old-fashioned way, and she had a specific way she liked everything done, from the angle in which the firewood was stacked to the way she peeled apples for pie. Those quirks were going to take some getting used to.

I snuggled back into the covers and tried to snooze some more, but finally motivated by my growling stomach, I headed into the kitchen for orange juice and toast. On the small dinette table Mae had left a note. Her perfect old-people cursive spilled across the back of a power bill envelope.

Going to town. Please split some more kindling and then have some fun in the garden. This afternoon we register you for school!

Love,
Mae

Hmm. Fun in the garden probably meant weeding.

I spent the next few hours chopping wood, with occasional breaks to throw a stick into the bushes for Katie. It wasn't too hard to make the kindling. It was just splitting the quartered rounds into smaller and smaller sticks you could use to start a fire.

As I worked, I tried to think of what my friends were doing now—well, what was left of them. Chelsea hadn't talked to me for weeks. I was sure she'd try to track me down when she learned that everything I'd finally told her about Matt was true. The last time we'd spoken I'd shown her the marks on my arms. She'd blamed them on softball and said that Matt had warned her I'd be spreading lies about him.

I zipped up my sweatshirt, feeling the slight chill of the gray September day. It was typical Pacific Northwest weather with a cloudy sky that looked ready to dump rain. If I was lucky, I had about an hour left of outdoor time before I'd be drenched. I focused on the task at hand, slamming down my hatchet into the wood, imagining for a brief second that I was bashing Matt. That was a little more satisfying than thinking it was just another chunk of fuel that would be used up in the stove when it got all cold out for real.

Bored with my diligent wood-chopping, Katie barked at me, picking up and dropping a stick I'd thrown a little while earlier. Though she was a gentle giant, she had a forceful bark. I set down the hatchet and chucked the stick as hard as I could into the woods. The dog tore after it into the trees, barking like crazy.

And then nothing. Her barking stopped. Weird.

"Katie!" I yelled, but she didn't come back. After a minute I followed her path. She'd run past the garden and into the woodlot behind. My feet tamped down cedar needles and moss as I moved through the trees. "Katie! Come!"

In a rush the shepherd whipped around a tree and almost bowled me over, then proudly dropped the stick and started barking again. Fine. The dog had a sense of humor.

"Hide-and-seek, huh? Awesome," I said.

She stopped barking and sat down in front of me, looking expectantly at the stick and then back at me. Then she repeated the stares. Stick. Me. Stick. Me. Stick.

"Okay. You win, girl." I picked up the stick and hurled it as far as I could. This time it zoomed past tree limbs and bushes, and Katie went nuts again, barking and dashing away after it, just a blur of brown and black against the late summer greens.

And then . . . again, the barking stopped.

"Katie!" I yelled. Playing along, I followed Katie's path through the trees and found myself at the edge of a big field, a field that smelled strongly of summer—of warm earth and mown grass. It was a beautiful meadow that I hadn't seen from Mae's backyard. A perfect rectangle framed by trees on three sides and dissolving into a mist on the other.

As I studied the meadow, Katie bounded toward me, carrying the stick in her mouth like a prize. I had to smile. I hadn't had a dog in years. When Mom and Dad were still married, we'd lived on the army base at Fort Lewis, south of Seattle, and had a little poodle named Tucker. He'd never been as much fun as Katie. Mostly, he'd wanted to chew shoes and chase the neighbor's Chihuahua. When Dad and Mom split up, Tucker had gone to live at a relative's house. Since then, Dad had been posted overseas, and Mom and I had lived in apartments, at least until we'd moved in with Pete. Pete was allergic to dogs and cats.

Dad was in Japan now, on an army base. Sometimes he sent me cool stuff for my birthday and usually he remembered to call on Christmas. It didn't bother me too much that he was so far away. I'd got used to Mom and me, and even Pete, being our own family. I hadn't thought about what it would be like to live without them nearby. In a way, it should have been harder than it seemed so far.

Then again, I hadn't really talked with Mom much this last year. She'd liked Matt, just like everyone had. And then when the truth about him came out—when it started showing on my body—she'd said she had never trusted him. She told me something had seemed off about Matt from the start, which was so easy to say in hindsight and didn't make me feel any better about what I'd been through.

I could still picture Mom's face the summer before last when I'd come home from Darcy Clegg's house party with a fat lip. Matt had thrown a full keg cup at me—just plastic, but with enough force to bruise my mouth. He'd apologized the whole way home, but meanwhile, my upper lip had puffed up and looked awful. I stood there in my mom's living room and lied about how it had happened. I told her I'd caught someone's elbow playing volleyball.

She'd known I was lying. I remember seeing it in her eyes. And I stood there wanting her to save me, to put a stop to something even I didn't feel I could stop. And she'd said nothing.

At the time, I'd told myself it was a good thing, that I should be glad she didn't pry. But looking back, it made me feel so sad.

It only got worse after that. Matt grabbing me—both hands on my upper arms—calling me names and shaking me when he got mad. Sometimes he apologized, but then other times he didn't—he'd just blame me for setting him off. And then that spring, Matt told me he'd break up with me if I didn't do *it*. Told me he'd find another girl who knew how to make him happy. Told me if I really loved him, I'd go through with it.

Afterward—after *it*—nothing had changed. Nothing, until my so-called best friend caught his eye a few weeks later. I felt so stupid. I went over and over it in my mind, trying to understand why I'd put up with all that he'd done to me—and what was worse, why I felt so sad when he'd gone off with Chelsea. It was dumb to even care.

I felt my breathing change. I was getting upset all over again, and I didn't want to cry anymore. I took a deep breath, focusing on the peaceful field. This place, this new start, was my escape. I never had to see him again.

Sitting up and panting in the grass, Katie was watching me. I could almost hear her dog ESP going, *Throw the stick already!*

"Okay. You win." I reached down and picked up Katie's skinny branch.

We played the game again, with me tossing the stick as hard as I could and Katie taking off. The wood cartwheeled against the white sky and then ended up on the other side of the field, just at the edge of the heavy mist. I wondered how there could still be an early-morning fog rolling in from somewhere. That kind of thing normally burned off by midday. Could there be a hidden creek?

I traced Katie's run, ending at the border of the mist. The air seemed dense, like winter when the air is heavy with dew and it's about to freeze. It was strange. Katie obediently stopped in front of me and dropped the stick at my feet. But I was distracted.

"Just a minute, pup," I said, walking into the coolness a little ways. I could feel it on my skin, like tiny cold crystals—a taste of winter when it was barely even fall.

Katie hadn't followed me. I backed out of the fog and found her waiting there. "Come on," I said, patting my leg, but she didn't come to me. She sat there, looking into the mist and panting. I called her again, and this time she whimpered.

"Fine."

Figuring I wasn't going to throw her the stick, Katie galloped away to chase after a bee. And I walked back into the misty clearing.

It was like the secret place of my suburban dreams. A thick cloud that swallowed up the day. That enveloped me. A perfect hiding place from the world. I breathed in the cool, cool air and walked forward a few more steps.

And then the weirdest thing happened. I heard something. Metallic. Rhythmic. Swishing like a machine. I was pretty sure Mae had said the closest neighbor was twenty acres away. This was all Mae's land. So where was the sound coming from?

I wandered farther into the mist toward the sound. But then I couldn't even see my hand anymore. I could hear Katie barking, but I couldn't make her out. And then Katie's bark faded. The metallic sound grew louder. *Swish. Swish.*

All at once I felt lost. The sun was blotted out by the whiteness all around. My heart beat faster as I turned in a slow circle, trying to get my bearings, and trying to see which way I had come into the fog. This was what it felt like to disappear, maybe. To lose yourself.

I ran in the opposite direction from the sound, panic forcing my pace. At last the strange noise faded and I was back in Mae's meadow, the mist behind me like a big white curtain. Katie ran up barking, sniffing me.

Walking back to the house, I stayed close to the dog, not sure what had happened in the clearing. Something was out there. Or maybe it was just me in the mist, lost forever.

I went back to the stump to split more kindling, the rhythm of my chopping and the clunk of the sticks hitting the pile on the ground comforting, familiar. Manual labor was the balm. Maybe disappearing was something I wasn't ready to do.

That afternoon, I rode along in Mae's truck as we drove up the main drag from the school, passing the town hall and library, the post office, and the feed store. Rockville wasn't exactly a sprawling metropolis—my new hometown was a retail strip and then miles of houses and farms. Maybe in Seattle I'd have been embarrassed by Mae's rusty vehicle, but jangling into a parking space at the town grocery, her truck was just another dirty pickup that needed a good hosing off and a paint job.

"Well, that was a nice surprise, wasn't it? I'm so glad they had room for you to enroll in some of the advanced classes," Mae said, turning off the engine.

"Yeah, it's fine," I said. I didn't really care what classes I took. My new high school was super small, just an old-fashioned brick building with hardwood floors that creaked. It wasn't anything like the newly built school I'd attended in Seattle, but Rockville High had a homey, friendly feeling to it, which was a good thing.

"The secretary showed me the transcript your mother had your old school send. You made some good grades the year before last," Mae said. She adjusted her hat and checked her reflection in the truck's rearview mirror.

"I did okay. Before." I shrugged. School used to be important to me. I'd even wanted to be a doctor or something, maybe. Now I didn't know what I was going to do after it all ended. Maybe I'd start out at community college and transfer somewhere. Maybe study psychology or something if I could get through the classes.

"Well, it's time for another chance at making those good grades, isn't it?" Mae said, patting me on the shoulder.

I managed a small smile for her. "Sure, Mae."

She grinned back and then glanced down at my tank top and jeans. "I meant to ask if you needed any school clothes." she asked gently. "There's not much here at the grocery, but we can take a trip down below this weekend."

"Down below?"

"That's what we call it when we drive to the big towns farther west as the Skagit River flows. It's not exactly Seattle, but there is a mall."

"I don't really need anything."

"Not even a blouse or two?" Mae asked. "It might be fun to go shopping."

"I don't really care what people think of what I wear," I said. "I'm not trying to prove anything."

"Yes, I think you favor your old Aunt Mae," she replied with a laugh. "I always wear the latest in overalls, though." She grabbed her oversize denim purse. "All right, now let's get some school supplies and a couple of big, juicy steaks. We'll have a nice cookout to celebrate your getting into *both* calculus and Creative Living."

"Yeah, *Creative* Living. I can't wait to start whipping up recipes based around refrigerator biscuits. It's great preparation for my adult life."

Mae winked. "There's the familiar sass. You're starting to acclimate, kid. By the time you get to school on Monday, you'll be back to your old self."

I'm sure Mae meant it in a good way. She didn't know I never wanted to be my old self ever again.

We entered the store, where the air conditioner was set to please a polar bear. The scents of the meat counter, bleachy disinfectant, freshly fried donuts, and overripe tomatoes hit my nose all at once. It was almost too much to take in. To top that, the place was packed with families with shopping carts full of groceries and dirty-faced toddlers. The cashiers did swift business while chattering over a scratchy-sounding country song piped through the PA system.

"You go pick out what you need for school, sweetie. Aisle five. I'll get the fixins for dinner."

Almost on autopilot, I moseyed away. I found the school supplies in the same aisle with Rockville High School T-shirts and lawn mower replacement parts. I browsed through the sweatshirts and tanks printed with a crowing rooster, and then moved on to finding what I really needed.

"I'd avoid the sparkly ones," said a tall boy, pointing down at the notebook in my hand. "If you get Mr. Sorenson for algebra, he'll mark your assignments down because of the glare."

"Thanks for the tip, but I don't have him."

"Ah—but you are new. So, let me guess—you're in trig, right? Then you have Miss Hammond. She appreciates sparkles."

I studied the guy. He had on a Rockville Roosters sweatshirt and running shorts and shoes. Short dark hair with wispy bangs framed his green eyes. Cute.

"I'm taking calculus," I said.

He looked impressed. "Ah-ha. In that case, we both have Mr. Agnew. He's neutral on sparkles. I'm Quinn. Quinn Hutchins."

"They let people name kids *Quinn* in this town?"

Quinn blinked at me. "Um, yeah. Why wouldn't they?"

"No, sorry, I just thought everyone would be, like, Jack or Billy or Bobby Ray."

"We're country, but we're not hicks," Quinn said, crossing his arms.

"So you're saying all Bobby Rays are hicks?" I replied.

"No. You're the one who—"

I held up a hand. "Kidding."

Just then a group of girls our age came giggling down aisle five. They were all dressed in Rockville High tees, shorts, and flip-flops. The blonde jingled keys in her hands.

"What's the deal?" she said, sidling up to Quinn. "We're supposed to grab some chips and go."

"Just saying hi to a newbie. What was your name?"

"Amy."

"Amy, nice to meet you," said the blonde in a bored voice. "I'm Melanie; this is Kristy, and Jane."

They all murmured their hellos and looked me up and down.

"I'd ask you along to the football team's barbecue, but my car only seats four," Melanie said with an apologetic look.

"No, it's all right. I have plans," I said with a shrug. Aunt Mae's backyard steaks sounded better than a barbecue with this girl.

"Okay. Later," Melanie said, moving away.

"Nice to meet you, Amy," Quinn said, following the group of girls down the aisle. "I'll see you next week—in class."

As they rounded the corner, Melanie flashed me a smirk that seemed more of a warning than a goodbye.

As if! I wanted to yell after her. I couldn't give two rats' butts about Quinn Hutchins, who wasn't even all that great. It almost made me laugh that even in a town as small as this one, high school clique stuff happened. And girls protected their stupid boyfriends who didn't give a crap about them.

Mae rounded the corner. "Are you ready to go?" she asked as I placed my items in her cart.

"Yes." I thought of the cool white mist in Mae's field. I thought of dissolving myself into it. Into the mist of not knowing. Of nothingness. Maybe it'd be a little scary, but wouldn't it be easier to turn invisible and not have to deal? I mean, why even get to know kids if they were going to be just the same as the ones I'd left?

Two days. I had two days until I had to start school. I closed my eyes on the way home, letting the wind cool my face and my frustration. This would be different, I promised myself. Nobody was going to wreck that for me.

I was calm. I could keep it together. And if not, there was always the mist.

CHAPTER TWO

Fresh apple pie. The crackle of dry leaves underfoot. Snowflakes. Those were the things Henry Briggs missed when he closed his eyes.

He could feel the summer sunshine on his face and smell the warm earth beneath his toes and the ripening strawberries in the nearby garden. Every day about this time, he heard the whir of dragonflies on their mission to the creek. It was familiar, but there was so much he would never know again—at least, he was pretty sure he wouldn't.

Lounging in the hammock strung between the cherry trees, he knew he had two hours before his mother would call him to the dinner table for Sunday supper—most likely ham and potato salad. And there was safety in that predictability. He shouldn't complain. He shouldn't tempt fate or God or whatever to take away the miracle he was living.

"Henry!" his grandfather called out from the side yard.

Yes, it was time to mow the lawn. The ever-greening blades of grass were ready again. Henry left his dog-eared copy of *Huckleberry Finn* in the hammock. He tucked his shirt in as he walked over to the shed, where Grandpa Briggs was rolling out the push mower.

"Oiled her up for you."

"Thank you, sir."

"Don't forget the path to the meadow," Grandpa said. "Won't be long before this June sunshine gives way to Old Man Winter and we're hauling in wood."

No, it won't give way. Though Henry didn't bother saying it aloud, he couldn't help thinking it.

Grandpa turned to go, but then paused. "Your mother's got dinner in the oven. She used our sugar ration to bake you a birthday cake. She went to a world of trouble over you. Don't dawdle."

"Yes, sir."

Grandpa Briggs gave him a pat on the shoulder as he passed.

Henry had tried, when this all had first come about, to talk to the old man about what was happening, but Grandpa had dismissed it as poppycock and sent him to do extra chores as punishment. Henry's mother, too, didn't seem to understand the miracle, so he had given up trying and didn't speak of it anymore.

So this now-familiar cycle continued. It began and ended and began again. His birthday came and went, another in the sea of early-summer days they floated upon. It was a safe sea, one that kept them protected from the awful, awful news that had come in late June the first time through.

The sun was high when Henry stopped at the edge of the meadow, hearing his grandfather calling. He left the mower on the side of the path to the clearing and ran toward the house, the flavor of the ham so familiar in his mouth, he could already taste it, along with the oniony potato salad. Oh, what he wouldn't give for a taste of late-fall elk roast or a Christmas cookie.

He'd realized long ago, though, that this life had its limitations, its boundaries. Keeping everyone alive meant that they couldn't simply hike into town and buy something else, or go to a neighbor's farm to trade them for something else. The mist hid them from the world in its protective folds. The mist was their end and their beginning.

All Henry had now was everything he'd had the summer his world had been destroyed. And that was all he was ever going to have again.

"Good grub," Grandpa Briggs said after dinner. He patted his belly as he sat back in his chair and let out a sigh.

"I have more," Mother said, emerging from the kitchen with a cake on a platter. In her usual blue housedress and slippers, she looked pretty but tired. It was hard to tell that his mother didn't feel well, but Henry knew she had spent most of the morning sleeping in her chair next to the radio. "Happy eighteenth birthday, son."

Henry did his best to put a surprised look on his face. "Thanks, Mother."

Mother eyed him as if she could tell he was faking. "Vanilla icebox was the best I could do. Don't you like that anymore?"

"Yes, it's still my favorite," Henry fibbed. He couldn't tell her after countless slices of the same birthday cake, it was getting tiresome.

Mother set the platter on the table and took a seat. She settled her napkin on her lap and then swept a few errant strands of her hair back up into its twist. "I'll make a chocolate cake when Robert comes home," she said, managing a smile. "Won't be long now that the boys have landed on the beaches over there."

"The Führer is on his last legs, that's for sure," Grandpa added.

Henry nodded, his lips pressed together, fighting the urge to tell them what would happen to his brother, what life had planned for the army private.

Mother glanced up at the calendar, where Henry's birthday was circled in red ink, June 14. "Summer's flying by. Don't you boys think he'll be home soon?"

"Yesiree, Robert might even come home in time to help hay," Grandpa said. "Johnson's got some good-looking fields this year. You boys could earn some good money."

Mother chuckled. "The last thing Robert is going to want to do is hay. He'll want to call on Rosie Grant and take her to the picture show."

"I think you're right." Grandpa struck a match, lit the single candle on Henry's cake, and slid the platter closer. "Now go on. Make a wish and we'll eat some of this delicious confection."

Henry blew out the candle, but he didn't make a wish. He never did. On all the birthdays he had lived, he had never made a wish.

Anyhow, a wish wasn't how all this began. It was a prayer he'd made a few days after his birthday, the night that the final telegram—and then the doctor—had come and gone. While his chums were dreaming of the adventures awaiting them overseas, Henry was kneeling at the side of his bed. As Henry had allowed himself tears in the dark, he'd prayed for a miracle.

A miracle wasn't the same thing as a wish. No birthday candle smoke could have wrought the life the Briggs family had been experiencing ever since that night.

"You go finish that mowing," Grandpa said. "I'll help your mother clean up."

The sweet taste of cake faded in Henry's mouth. "Yes, sir." He left his plate and napkin on the table and pushed his chair carefully into the table. He would mow, and the rest of the day would unfold as the others of this summer always had.

The grass in the clearing at the edge of their meadow was tall. Despite the sun, the clearing was filled with mist as usual.

Henry had tried once in the beginning to travel through the mist, to see what was on the other side. After all, the mist hadn't been there until the morning after his prayer. But as he had approached the far edge of the clearing, the mist had thickened into a white dense fog he couldn't see through. And he'd heard a strange humming noise. That's when he'd realized it was a boundary. It was the very edge of the Briggs farm property and perhaps the edge of something bigger.

Henry had never gone that far into the mist again. He'd never dared, lest something happened and he couldn't return. He couldn't bear to think of what that might do to his family. He didn't know what would happen to them if he weren't there to do what he'd always done—pray that the miracle would continue for another day—and that was infinitely scarier than the idea of getting lost.

He pushed the mower, clipping the grass with a metallic swish-swish. He stopped at the side of the path, stooping to pick up some rocks he always seemed to find, and toss them away into the mist. It had taken only a few times of rolling over the rocks and having to spend the rest of the afternoon sharpening mower blades for him to remember. As boring as it was, Henry was good at mowing this stretch of the land.

He paused to scratch his leg. Mother would probably have lemonade ready by the time he made it back to the house. She'd be sipping a glass out on the porch and listening to the radio music drifting out through the open window. Some days he joined her, and on others he sipped cool water in the shade.

He was behind schedule—it had to be about four in the afternoon, judging by the sun. There was still raking to do, and then his grandfather would need him to help with the garden chores after supper that evening.

Henry wiped his sweat-beaded forehead with the back of his forearm, the heat really getting to him. Wanting to cool off a bit, he left the mower on the side of the path and stepped into the clearing, arms outstretched so the tiny water droplets in the air could hit his skin full force. He ran forward, as far as he dared, and the mist of the clearing chilled him instantly. He let out a huge sigh. And then he heard a voice.

Henry froze.

"Hey!" A girl's voice came again, cutting through the mist.

Henry didn't know what to do, so he stood there pretending he was invisible.

It didn't work. A girl walked toward him in the mist—a girl in dungarees and some kind of an athlete's jacket zipped over a man's undershirt. It was a strange ensemble to be sure, since Henry was used to seeing girls in blouses and skirts at school. Usually girls in trousers were gardening or doing factory work.

"Hey," she said. "Um, what was that noise?"

"I beg your pardon, please?" Henry blinked at the girl. He was almost tempted to think she was some kind of angel, but no angel he'd ever heard of looked like her. Maybe she was a ghost? Or maybe she was from the Wilsons' place, the next farm over, and had found a way to breach the boundary of the clearing.

"I heard a sound. Like a machine. I was wondering what it was. Or maybe it was nothing. Did you hear it?" the girl said, stopping a few feet from him. Henry felt her stare move over his work boots, suspendered pants, and short-sleeved, button-up shirt.

"I was mowing," Henry said with a shrug.

"It wasn't a gas mower I heard," the girl said.

"I use a push mower."

"Really?" she said. "That sucks. Maybe you can borrow Aunt Mae's lawn tractor. You know her, right? She lives just over there."

Henry didn't know who Aunt Mae was, but he wasn't sure he should tell this strange girl anything. "Thank you, kindly. My mower's fine."

"Okay," the girl said. "Well, I guess I'll leave you alone."

"Wait," he said, not wanting her to go just yet. "Where are my manners? I'm Henry. It's nice to meet you." He almost reached out a hand to shake, but then he realized if this girl was some kind of apparition, he wouldn't be able to touch her. He was curious, but at the same time, he didn't want to find out. He stuck his hands in his pockets.

"Amy," the girl said. "Maybe I'll see you on the school bus on Monday."

"Monday?"

"Yeah. You know, it's the first day of school—Monday, September tenth?"

"September," he said, rolling the word around in his mouth.

"Yeah. Can't you feel the chill in the air?" she said.

"Sure," Henry lied.

"What's up with this mist?" she said. "It's odd, don't you think?"

"Ah . . . yes, I suppose it's a bit peculiar."

Amy regarded Henry again and then said, "I kinda like the way it feels. Like you're hiding from the rest of the world. Is that why you're out here, too?"

"Sure, I suppose." He hadn't thought of it quite that way, but hiding was precisely what the clearing was helping his family do.

"Okay, well, see ya. I've got to go," Amy said, turning away.

"So long. Perhaps I'll see you again," Henry said, his voice tinged with hope. "Say, before you run off—will you tell me where you came from?" he said, hazarding a real question.

"Over there." Amy backed away into the mist. "Bye."

Henry waved as she disappeared to someplace where it was September. And suddenly, even though it had been a strange meeting, he felt comforted. Possibly, he'd made his first friend in a long, long while—whoever she was.

Whenever she was.

CHAPTER THREE

Mae cut me a slice of apple pie and then one for herself. "Ice cream, Amy?"

"Yeah, please."

She dipped us each up a scoop, and then we took our plates to the back porch. After a long day of chopping and weeding, I was ready for a well-earned rest and a piece of homemade pie. And I kept thinking about the clearing and that boy Henry with his way old-school farmer outfit. I didn't think people still dressed like that in the country—I mean, the kids in town I'd met wore the same kind of stuff as the kids back in the city. But maybe Henry was in some kind of religious group that didn't believe in new technology and homeschooled all their kids. He seemed different, that was for sure.

"Mae, do any families live close by?" I didn't want to come out and ask her about a guy I'd met. I didn't want to go there.

"Well, the nearest neighbors are the Taylors down the road." Mae took a seat in one of the rockers and spread a paper napkin across her lap. "If you like, we'll ride over there one day so you can meet them. They have a daughter about your age—Lori. She plays soccer on the school's team." Mae gestured toward my plate. "How do you like it?"

I took a bite of pie. The crust was crumbly and buttery and the apples tart on my tongue. "Good," I said.

"Just good?" Mae raised her eyebrows.

"It's *excellent*," I said, helping myself to another bite. "So, they just have Lori, huh? No brothers?" I asked.

Mae set down her fork. "Sweetie, is that really what you should be worried about? After what your mother told me . . ."

"No, no. It's not like that," I said, holding up a hand. "It's *so* not that, Mae. Don't worry. I'm not looking for a boyfriend anytime soon."

Mae let out a relieved sigh and her stern look softened. "That's good. As long as you're here, I want you to be free to make your own choices, but I won't sit idly by while you get yourself hurt again."

"What did Mom say?" I asked, mashing a piece of pie crust with my fork.

"Enough. I wanted to understand the situation. It's hard to be old, let alone old and living with a teenager. I wanted to make an informed decision about having you come to live with me."

"That's fair," I said, though the possibility that Mae would have said no to my coming here had never even occurred to me before. But then again, maybe I would have done the same thing— wondered why anyone young would want to live in a country trailer with an elderly auntie.

"Let's make an agreement," Mae said after she'd finished off her slice of pie. "Let's promise to tell each other the truth even if it's hard."

"Okay. I'll try."

"No trying, only doing," Mae said.

I shrugged and we shook on it.

"So, about the boys around here . . ."

Mae let out an exasperated sigh. "You'll meet the boys in town at school on Monday. Then you can ask me all the questions in the world." She picked up our empty plates and patted me on the shoulder as she passed me on the way to the kitchen.

I wiped the pie crumbs from my mouth and stared out at the woodlot. Beyond there, the mist of the clearing was probably dis-

sipating, dissolving back into the night sky. And out there somewhere was that guy Henry. I hoped Mae was right. Maybe I'd see
him at school. It would be nice to start off the year knowing one
person who didn't seem to be a jerk.

I went back into the house, Katie following right on my heels.
Did I actually have a reason to look forward to Monday? I couldn't
even believe that myself.

My enthusiasm for school faded quickly. I really wanted to be
a new me, but I didn't want to have to talk about myself, and in
every stinking class the teacher made me stand and give the class
my life story. By noon on Monday, everyone in school knew my
name and where I was from. I was officially *the new girl*.

At lunch, I took one of the few vacant seats in the small cafeteria, where every single person in my classes seemed to be eating
all at one time. In my old school, there were four different lunch
periods, so the kids were staggered in groups. Here, there was
only one for the high schoolers. Earlier in the day, the junior high
school kids used the room, so the tables were good and messy by
the time we got there. But almost making up for that, the food
was served up by two nice ladies, who asked me my name and
then gave me extra french fries as a welcome.

The chicken sandwich was all right, though maybe a little
chewy and glopped with too much mayo. I took another bite and
chewed thoughtfully while I tried not to pay attention to the fact
that everyone at the table was sneaking looks at me. Then I saw
the boy from the grocery store stroll into the lunchroom, Melanie
and her friends trailing behind him in a giggling bunch.

The dark-haired boy next to me must have noticed my stare.
"Quinn Hutchins," he said.

"Yeah, I met him."

Over in line, Quinn caught my eye and waved. I gave him a half smile and went back to sipping my pop.

The boy next to me paused in midbite of his sandwich and said, "I've known him since he was in preschool. He's not all that great."

"I think he's hot," said a small girl across the way. "You know, we're neighbors," she said, gesturing at me with her fork. "You and me. Not me and Quinn—he lives out on Russell Road. You live at Mae's place."

The boy snorted. "Lori. Information overload. Give the girl a chance to get used to us. In the city, that's called stalking, right?" He took another bite of sandwich.

"Well, I'm from Seattle, if that's what you mean by city. It's not like I lived in a high rise or something," I replied with a shrug. I glanced over at Lori, who with her mousy brown hair in a sloppy ponytail and a sprinkling of freckles across the bridge of her nose, looked like she belonged a few grades below us. "It's nice to meet you. I'm Amy. My aunt told me about you."

"I know. She called my dad and asked me to sit with you at lunch." Her cheeks went red. "Oops. I wasn't supposed to say that. Sorry."

The boy barely stifled a laugh.

"I would've sat next to you on the bus, but my mom gives me a ride in the mornings. She's Suzi, the lunch lady with the blond hair," Lori said. "It's not so cool to have your mom be a lunch lady, but sometimes she gives me an extra cookie."

"I just met her. She's really nice," I said. "And for the record, I didn't take the bus this morning, either."

"Smart." The boy wiped his mouth with a napkin. "I'm Jackson, by the way."

"Lori's PR coach, right?" I asked around a bite of fry.

He cracked a smile. "I like to think of myself as more of a handler."

Lori crunched a carrot dipped in ranch dressing. "So, you got a ride to school? That's good. Wait till you ride the bus home today—it takes forever down the back roads."

"Oh, great." I was suddenly glad Mae had insisted on driving me that morning. As the truck idled in the crowded parking lot, she'd hugged me and then tucked a few wrinkled bills in my hand for lunch. As Mae pulled away, I had barely resisted the urge to run after her truck. Instead, I'd sucked it up and walked toward the school steps. This was what I had wanted. So why did I feel so scared?

"So, have you met anyone else?" Lori asked.

"Um, just a kid named Henry, who lives near us."

Jackson shook his head. "Never heard of him."

"Well, maybe I'm not the only new one this year," I murmured. "You guys are both seniors. You probably know all the kids in school, right?"

"Yep, I'm a lifer. Can't you tell?" asked Jackson.

"I don't know. I just got here."

Jackson grinned at my sarcasm. "Everyone in this lunchroom—no, wait, we had a couple newbies last year—so everyone but *three* people in this lunchroom has known each other since they were potty-trained."

"Most people are pretty cool," said Lori. "You're going to fit right in."

"Yeah," I mumbled. I wasn't sure I wanted to fit in.

"It must be way different than Seattle," Jackson said. "Your old school must have been pretty big, huh?"

"Yeah." I dragged a few fries through the extra mayo from the sandwich and scanned the room for Henry, wondering if he was having the same experience that I was.

Lori squished another blob of dressing onto her lunch tray and dunked a celery stick. "So, how come you're not in my classes so far? Don't you have Garner for English?"

"No, I have Mills. After lunch."

"Advanced Placement English—nice," said Jackson. "Me, too. I'll walk you there." He gave me a broad, confident smile.

I felt my shoulders tense up. I was suddenly aware that Jackson was kind of cute, kind of big, and definitely a guy. He was still grinning in a trust-me-I'm-in-charge kind of way.

"Um. That's okay. I can probably find it."

"It's no trouble," said Jackson, balling up his napkin and throwing it on his tray. "I'll accompany you."

"I said no." My voice came out weird. Harsh.

Jackson gave me an odd look. "Oh—kay. I'll just see you there."

"Geez. Sorry, I didn't mean anything. I'm just, you know, independent."

He shrugged and got up with his lunch tray. "Suit yourself."

Lori, who'd watched the interchange silently, took a last sip of milk and eyed me with a funny look. "Well—see you around, I guess," she said, walking off with her tray.

I released the breath I'd been holding. I needed to chill if I wanted to make any friends in this place. Jackson was just being nice—and he wasn't Matt. I chewed a bite of oatmeal cookie and pictured the cool, calm mist of the clearing. I tried to remember what Mae had told me last night before I went to bed, my stomach a ball of nerves. *This too shall pass.* Right.

When the bell for class rang, I realized I was the only student left in the cafeteria. As I dumped the contents of my tray, the lunch ladies gave me a sympathetic look and a wave of their plastic-gloved hands.

"How was your first day?" Mae took my backpack from me and slung it over one shoulder.

I watched the bus roll off down the road toward Lori's stop. She hadn't sat by me on the ride home, and I didn't blame her. When she'd turned up in my gym class that afternoon, I'd tried to be friendly, but maybe the damage was already done. I'd come off mean or crazy or something in the lunchroom. I hoped that first impression would wear off.

"It was okay," I said, turning back to Mae. I'd promised her I'd always tell the truth, but I didn't want to rehash the horrible day. "It's going to be fine, I guess."

"It takes a while to make friends," Mae said. "You have to be patient with yourself."

Katie trotted up the driveway toward us, hope in her eyes and a stick in her mouth. I gave her a pat, but I didn't go for the stick.

Mae squinted at me. "Don't be too hard on yourself, sweetie. You survived day one. That's a start."

"Yeah, *survived* is a good word." I stopped, noticing Mae was slowing her walk. "Here, you don't have to carry that backpack, Mae."

"I'm old, but I'm tough," she said, but she handed the bag to me. "Judging by the weight of those books, you have a lot of homework."

"Some," I said.

She sucked in a deep breath and leaned against the handrail of the stairs. "Well, I hope it's not too much. We have beans to can."

"Cans of beans?"

Mae chuckled. "Amy, every family in the valley cans. In fact, we're running behind. We have a bushel of late green beans from our neighbor Lawrence's garden to do tonight. I want to make some sauce out of our Jonagolds, and of course we'd best make some jam out of those blackberries before they're all gone to the birds."

"Mmm . . . your jam," I said.

"It's *our* jam this year. Won't it be nice to give your mom a jar for Christmas?"

Mom. I hadn't talked to her since the first night I came to Mae's. I just nodded at my aunt.

Kindness crinkled at the corners of her eyes. "I didn't mean to make you sad. You must really miss her."

"Yeah," I said, truthfully.

"Hard to tell. You've been awfully quiet," Mae said. "Did you know when you were young, you were a regular chatterbox? I could barely get a word in edgewise."

We climbed the stairs together and I followed Mae into the kitchen. Big bowls of freshly picked green beans filled the table. After we washed our hands, Mae handed me a paring knife. On the back porch, she showed me how to pull the string of each bean, clip off both of the ends, and then cut the beans into three equal pieces.

We worked silently, the only sounds the tink-tink of the wind chimes in the garden, the growly sound of Katie gnawing on a stick, and the ding of the beans dropping into the giant bowl between us.

Finally Mae said, "So, did you have your questions answered about the boys in town today?"

I rolled my eyes. "Not even on my radar, Mae."

"Never much on mine, either," she said. "Always preferred my own company."

"Well, there was one boy," I admitted. "From the other day—a Henry. You ever heard of him?"

Mae raised her eyebrows at me. "Henry? Now that's a throwback. A real old-fashioned name."

"Yeah, well, I met one. About my age. He lives near here," I said, deliberately being vague. I didn't want to get Henry in trouble for trespassing, if that's what he was doing. "He wasn't at school, though."

Mae threw some cut beans into the big blue bowl between us. "So this boy caught your eye?"

I shrugged. "He seemed nice. And kinda different. A real farm boy, I guess. And not pushy."

"The young men today can be pushy," Mae said.

I snipped off some green bean ends. "Yeah. That boy Matt, the one Mom probably told you about . . . he was way too pushy."

"Then good riddance."

"Yeah." I don't know why, but my voice sounded weak. It *was* good riddance to be free of Matt, but why did it seem like I didn't believe it? Maybe I was still mixed up about the whole thing.

Watching me, Mae set down her paring knife and stretched out her cramped fingers. "You never settle for a boy like Matt again. You hear me? You're a special girl."

"Yeah."

"I mean it. You are special. When you were little and I came to see you during the Holidays, you'd show me all your papers from school. They were covered with stars. So many stars. And you'd be so proud. 'Look at this A on my math test!' you'd shout. You were also quite an artist. I could barely get in the door without you bombarding me with drawings you'd made."

"I did that?" I said, barely remembering any of it.

"And then it all stopped," Mae said. "You turned about eleven and it stopped."

"Dad and Mom . . ."

"Yes, that was about the time they split up," she said. "That was really hard for you, sweetie."

"It wasn't that bad," I said.

Mae shook her head. "It was pretty bad."

"I don't remember that."

"Of course not, you were a child." Mae paused. "Your poor mother, she did the best she could."

I cut a few more beans and tossed them into the bowl. "I guess. She worked a lot when they got divorced."

"She was terrified," Mae said slowly. "Worried about how she was going to be both parents for you. But the thing she didn't do—didn't have the knowledge or the time to do—was to remind you that you are special."

"I'm just a normal girl."

"No, no. You're special. And I'm sorry I didn't help your mother remind you of that. I should have had you spend summers with me in the valley. I guess I had the feeling that it would've been too boring for you with just old me to keep you company, but now I see it might have done us both some good." Mae reached out and patted me on the back. There were tears in her eyes. "If I could go back in time, Amy, I'd give that gift to you—and I'd remind you that you're special every time I could. Not just when I showed up with a jar of jam with a bow on top."

I felt my throat clog up. "Mae. Seriously. It's all right."

"No," Mae said. "It's never all right to forget something that important."

I concentrated on the beans, stringing, clipping, and then cutting them into chunks. I didn't like seeing Mae upset. And I didn't really get what she was saying. She was talking as if everyone were supposed to be going around thinking about how special they were all the time. But I thought everyone was supposed to be all the same. It didn't seem very cool to be thinking you're better than anyone else.

We worked on the beans until around sunset, and Mae served us some chili she'd been cooking in her Crock-pot all day. Then we turned on the TV, and I did my homework on the floor next to Katie, who snored, paws twitching in her sleep. I felt safe—almost.

This was my new family, my new life. It was going to be okay, and I was pretty sure my plan to forget about everything back home would work. The only problem I had now was figuring out how to get through school. And how to make a friend.

CHAPTER FOUR

From the moment Henry opened his eyes, she'd been on his mind. *Amy*. Her name was Amy, he reminded himself. She hadn't come back to the clearing so far, but he hoped she would today.

As sunlight hit the kitchen windows, he cleaned his plate in short order, wiping up the last of the sausage gravy with a piece of biscuit. He actually never got tired of his mother's breakfasts. He would happily eat her biscuits for a lifetime.

"You in a hurry?" Grandpa Briggs asked, pouring cream into his second cup of coffee. "You seem to have ants in your pants this morning."

"No, sir." Henry took another biscuit from the towel-lined basket. Maybe just one more with some of the strawberry preserves.

Mother sat down across from Grandpa, drying her hands on her apron. "You're a good eater today," she said, watching Henry doctor up the biscuit with the jam. Her own plate was empty. Her appetite was weak, as it always was.

"I have a full morning ahead," Henry said. "Big list of chores."

His grandfather snorted. "Most of the summer you've been lazing in the hammock! To what do we owe this burst of enthusiasm?"

Henry took a bite of the biscuit, savoring the sweet fruit topping. He hadn't had any jam in a week of breakfasts, just for a change. "Need to finish that mowing," he said.

"Thought you finished that already," said Grandpa.

"Always more that needs mowing," Henry replied.

"So no more communing with Mr. Twain under a shady tree?" Mother said, managing a smile.

"Well, I might read some Faulkner today," he said.

"You had enough *Huckleberry Finn* already?" Grandpa asked.

"Yes, sir," Henry said. In truth he'd gone through the entire Briggs library several times over. He finished the last bite of the biscuit and wiped his mouth with the embroidered napkin. "May I be excused, please?"

His mother raised her eyebrows. "Of course, dear."

Grandpa tipped his cup. "We need to cut some of that lettuce today."

"I'll do it after I mow, sir," Henry said. "In fact, I'll go get started on that grass now before it gets too warm outside." He took his plate and set it in the sink.

"Don't know what's got into that boy," Grandpa murmured as Henry walked out of the kitchen, heading straight for the back field.

How long could he pretend to mow the path to the clearing? So far, the careful mowing had not paid off. He'd taken his time, rolling over and over the same section of perfect green, and still no Amy.

It was a few hours after dinner now, and his belly was full of the leftover ham and cake. He was ready for a rest. Henry pulled his copy of *The Sound and the Fury* out of his back pocket and lay down beside the mower. He was strategically positioned along the edge of the mist, about twenty yards from where he'd seen Amy the other day.

"Through mowing for the day?"

Henry was startled to see his grandfather walking toward him.

Grandpa never came out to check up on him—it wasn't at all his normal pattern. The old man slowed his walk and took off his hat to fan himself.

Henry sat up in the grass. "Just taking a break."

"I see. Well, don't forget about the lettuce. Your mother's going to have supper ready in a few hours, and she wants you to bring in some greens for the salad."

"Yes, sir. I'll do it." Henry picked up his book, expecting the conversation was over.

Grandpa stood there, giving him a funny stare. "Eerie out here, don't you think, Henry? Wouldn't you be more comfortable in the hammock? That's your normal library."

"I felt like relaxing in the grass, Grandpa. It's only a short break," Henry said. "I'm going back to it in just a moment."

"Well, when you complete this path, you have the entire lawn near the house. Not sure why you'd want to work out here in the back in this foggy swamp."

Henry shrugged. "I know, sir. It's just that I'm trying to finish the part of the job I skimped on the other day."

"All right, then. I'll call you for supper. Don't fall asleep out here. If your mother doesn't get her salad greens after while, she'll be awfully disagreeable." Grandpa Briggs walked off, shaking his head.

Henry read a few more pages until the grasshoppers, stirred up by the mowing, started interrupting. After swatting a few of the critters away, Henry got up and carried his book to a stump farther inside the cool mist. He lost himself in the story, reading about Benji and his family.

And then, a voice cut across the clearing. "Hey!"

He looked up to see Amy moving toward him in the curtain of mist. He smiled, setting his book on the stump. "Hello. I wondered if you'd come back."

"Yeah, well, here I am, I guess."

Henry studied Amy. Long brown hair, deep brown eyes, her eyelids painted with sparkly silver makeup. She'd be even prettier in a fancy dress at a high school dance, or in a colorful skirt and blouse, but, Henry noted, again Amy wore dungarees and a plain undershirt. This one was blue and printed with the words OLD NAVY. He didn't understand why such a pretty girl wore such plain, masculine clothes.

"You know someone in the service?" he said, pointing at her shirt.

Amy gave him a disbelieving look. "Um, my dad's in the army. But this is from the store—you know, Old Navy?"

Henry stared hard at the shirt's printing. "Never heard of it."

"Well, they're kind of everywhere. Don't you ever go to the city to shop?"

"We don't need to leave the farm," Henry said carefully.

"Yeah, I didn't see you at school yesterday or today."

"That's right. You went to school," Henry said. The idea of school seemed very unreal to him. He'd liked high school, had been a good student, and got along well with his teachers and friends. He missed the challenge of learning new things and the thrill of throwing out a runner on first when he pitched for the Rockville Roosters baseball team. His classes seemed so far away.

"Are you homeschooled or something?" she asked.

"*Homeschooled*—you mean tutored?"

"Yeah, I guess. Supposedly there are a few kids in the valley who are."

Henry sat down on the stump. "I don't go to school right now. I'm helping out my family."

"Oh. That's cool, I guess." She took a seat on the grass next to the stump and then reached out toward his pant leg. "Hold still."

Henry froze. "What are you—"

She touched him, brushing against his shin and coming away with a large grasshopper. She leaned over and gently set the bug in the tall grass on the other side of her.

"Much obliged," Henry said, stunned. He didn't tell her that he was glad to know she wasn't a ghost or angel. At least, he didn't think they'd be able to touch if she were.

"You're welcome," Amy said, wrinkling her nose.

"What's the matter?" he said.

"It's just—*much obliged?* That's some real country talk you've got there, Henry." She gave him a warm smile that made a blush rise in Henry's cheeks.

"Oh. Well, I do live in the country," he said, glancing over at the tall grass, where the grasshopper had struck up a chirping song.

"Hey—shhh." Amy took a seat on the ground near him, an expression of delight brightening her face.

Henry shook his head. It wasn't unusual to encounter insects traveling through the clearing, especially grasshoppers and bumblebees. Rarely, though, had he seen a bird. They seemed to sense that things were different here. Maybe it was that the winds and sun felt strange. Certainly, the breeze moved slower across this part of the field and the sky was farther away, hidden by the mists.

When the grasshopper's song ended, Amy plucked a blade of the long grass and twirled it in her fingers. "Wasn't that pretty?"

Henry watched her pull the strands of the grass apart. "Haven't you ever heard a grasshopper chirp before?"

"Not really. I guess I never paid much attention to that stuff before. Not too many grasshoppers on my old lawn, anyway."

"Plenty round here," said Henry.

"I bet." She looked at him with those big brown eyes—like chocolate with flecks of gold.

Henry was suddenly aware of the time that must have elapsed since he'd started talking with Amy. "Excuse me, but I have to get along now," he said, rising from the stump. "Mother's expecting me to bring in some vegetables from the garden for supper. I'll catch heck if I'm late."

"Catch heck?" Amy said. "Wow. I wouldn't want that to happen."

"You ain't kidding."

"Right. I gotta go, anyway," Amy said, her gaze dropping to her hands. "Homework. It was, um, cool to see you again."

"Maybe our paths will cross again?"

"Yeah, maybe." She backed away into the mist, giving him a little wave.

"So long, Amy," he called. He tucked his book into his pocket and dragged the mower out of the clearing.

As Henry hurried toward the garden, his heart felt alive with a feeling that'd been absent for a while: hope. He was full of the hope that she'd come to the clearing again.

It was so wonderful to have someone to talk to. And even though he wasn't sure it was right, he couldn't help wanting something more than another aimless string of summer days—something different.

And the fact that she was a beautiful girl didn't hurt at all.

"You were acting strangely earlier," Grandpa Briggs said, settling down into his rocking chair on the porch later that evening. He looked out across the garden, toward the road that led into town. "You feeling better now?"

"I'm feeling fine," Henry said. "Nothing a slice of Mother's icebox cake couldn't cure," he joked. But he wasn't fine. He hadn't been fine since he'd caught sight of Amy.

"Alma makes a grand cake," his grandfather conceded. "She's as good a baker as her mother ever was. She can't beat your grandmother's cornbread, though. So light, so tender."

Henry nodded. One of his earliest memories was his grandmother feeding him cornbread dripping with honey. She and Grandpa had been young when they'd built this house, barely older than Henry. But Grandma had been gone many years.

Grandpa turned his head toward the sound of the radio's soft music. "Say, your mother looked better this morning," he said. "Had more color in her cheeks."

Henry sighed. He couldn't count the number of times his grandfather had said those words in an attempt to whitewash what they both felt, both knew in their hearts. Tonight, though, he abandoned his standard reply. "She's not better, sir."

Grandpa gave him a disapproving look. "Why on earth would you say such a thing?"

Henry paused, wondering the same thing himself. Still, he felt compelled to go on. "She's sick."

"Dr. Morris said it's normal for women to be fatigued from time to time."

"Mother's in pain," Henry said. "It's not only fatigue. I wish the doctor could have done more for her before it was too late."

"What do you mean by that?" his grandfather demanded.

Henry couldn't bring himself to broach the subject, to even suggest what Mother might do, what she *would do* if the summer ended. "She's in a great deal of pain," he repeated.

Grandpa went back to rocking. "All of us live in pain, Henry. That's the human condition. Some pain you can see from the outside, and some is buried deep on the inside. We all have our crosses to bear."

Henry studied his grandfather's weathered face. "I haven't heard you quote the Good Book in a while."

"You know my daddy was a preacher back east in the Carolinas," Grandpa said. "I had quite a dose of the Bible growing up."

"Did you ever stop believing?"

His grandfather let out a breath. "No, young man, that, I did not do. The world turns because of the Lord. The fact that we live each day is a miracle. A gift."

"A gift that people take for granted," Henry said.

"Have you been into those philosophy books again?" Grandpa said, allowing himself a laugh.

"Not today, sir," Henry said. He'd read through all of them so many times he didn't think there were many mysteries of the universe left to unravel.

"The world is a complicated place," Grandpa said. He put a hand on Henry's shoulder. "We all do our best." Grandfather surveyed Henry's eyes. "You surely do seem different tonight. You certain you're feeling well?"

"Yes, sir." Henry got up and walked to the edge of the porch, facing the clearing.

"Maybe you're growing up," Grandfather said. "You're older now—soon you'll be a man like Robert, fighting the good fight."

Henry gripped the railing. Yes, that was the unspoken topic at the table that evening: that in the real summer, if it were allowed to continue, the letter from the draft board requesting him to report would most likely come. That within days he would take his place with the other boys of Rockville who were shipping out to the armed forces. He'd be a man like Robert, a man prepared to die for his country. A man who maybe wouldn't make it home at all.

"The summer's only just begun. That's not for a while yet," his grandfather said. "Don't you worry."

"Yes, sir," said Henry. Then he excused himself. There were prayers to be said. Futures to hold off. Lives right there on the farm to protect.

CHAPTER FIVE

Over the next few days at school, my mind kept returning to the clearing with Henry. How peaceful the time seemed there with him, and how different he seemed from the rest of the people in Rockville. He didn't ask a lot of questions, and he didn't seem to want anything from me. It felt restful to be with him, talking in the field with the cool mist, all the while the grasshoppers singing, and a stray dragonfly buzzing through the fog like a little helicopter. It was like a dream.

Rockville High's Creative Living class, on the other hand, was not a dream. Ms. Grady had just finished presenting a lecture about nutrition and was now walking us through a recipe for "homemade" pizza that involved store-bought biscuit mix and a jar of spaghetti sauce. When she called for us to find a partner, I looked up to see Quinn moving purposefully toward me across the room of kitchenettes.

"Hey." Jackson popped up in front of me, holding out two aprons. "How about it?" he said. "The pizza toss is my best event."

"Uh . . ." I stuttered. I was focused on Quinn, who had started over to me and now made a sudden turn toward Melanie's friend Jane. The two of them laughed as they helped each other tie on the aprons.

"Oh," Jackson said, noticing my stare. "You were hoping for pretty boy over there."

"No, it's fine." Truthfully, I was glad Jackson was giving me another chance.

"Well, then," he said, "shall we?"

"Yeah, thanks." I took one of the aprons from him and put it on.

He donned his with a goofy flourish, finishing it with a dopey bow around his middle. "How do I look?"

"Awesome." I laughed as he retied the apron the right way. "Look, Jackson, I'm sorry about the other day in the lunchroom. I'm not used to people wanting to help me do stuff and asking me questions."

He raised an eyebrow. "Yeah, but you're new. How else are people supposed to get to know you?"

I shrugged. "Yeah. Well, thanks for trying to make me feel welcome, anyway."

"No prob."

Jackson got out the measuring cup and started dumping the baking mix into the large metal bowl at our station. Meanwhile, I got out the milk and pizza toppings. We worked quickly, following Ms. Grady's lame-o recipe to a T.

"Plain cheese okay?" Jackson asked, after we'd spooned the red sauce over the pressed-down crust.

"Yeah, with extra pepperoni and sausage," I said.

Jackson paused, his hands full of shredded mozzarella. "Amy, I'm a vegetarian," he said.

"Yeah, right," I said, giggling.

"I'm serious," he said.

My mouth dropped open. "A vegetarian? You guys raise cattle up in the valley."

"My family doesn't. My mom's an ecologist for the forest service. My sister and I are both vegetarians like Mom. We have a big organic garden."

"Okay, now I've heard everything."

Jackson started sprinkling the cheese on the crust. "You think it's all loggers and ranchers in Rockville, but there are other folks, too. Everyone's different, but I guarantee you, we're mostly civilized if you take the chance to get to know us."

"So, you're veggie. Does the store in town even have tofu?"

He snorted out a laugh. "There's more to vegetarian cooking than tofu, but yes, they do carry it down at the store."

I shook my head at him. "Who knew?"

"You never know until you ask." Jackson wiped his hands on a towel and surveyed our sad-looking pizza, which was misshaped and heaped with way too much cheese. He opened the preheated oven and slipped the pan inside, showing me his fingers were crossed. "In fact, after school today, I'll give you a ride home and we can swing by the garden, just in case you don't believe me. My mom's got some giant pumpkins out there. They're pretty impressive."

The thought of being in a car alone with Jackson felt a little scary to me. Trapped in a close space with a boy I didn't know if I could trust. Trapped with no other way home if he decided to stop somewhere. My face burned. "Um . . . I have to study at the library."

"Okay," Jackson said slowly. "Well, maybe some other time, then. I drive every day."

I busied myself washing my hands. After a moment, I broke the uncomfortable silence. "So, is there anything else I should know about this valley?"

"Hmm. Let me think on that one. How about you? Any good tales from the city? What's it like living down there?"

I felt my hands tense up. "It's different."

"That bad, huh?" he said, then added with a small smile, "Oh, and there I go nosing into your business."

"What business is that?" Quinn walked up, wiping a smear of pizza sauce from his hands onto his apron.

Jackson got a little red in the cheeks and backed up a step.

"Hi, Quinn," I said. "How's your pizza coming?"

"It's going to be delicious," Quinn said, his eyes twinkling.

Jackson started plunking bowls and spoons into our water-filled sink. Obviously, he wasn't pleased.

"If we teamed up, I bet we could've made an Italian masterpiece," said Quinn, peeking skeptically through the oven window at our handiwork.

"Hmm, that I doubt," I said. "Real pizza involves yeast and flour and rising time. My mom used to bake it with me when I was a kid."

"Quinn!" Jane snapped from over at their station, "I'm not doing your dishes!"

"Women." Quinn shrugged. "See you around, Amy."

"Why don't you like him?" I asked Jackson when we were alone.

"What's *to* like? You must have had guys like Quinn at your school. His type's pretty common."

"Yeah, I guess." But Jackson was right. Of course we had guys like Quinn at my old school. Every boy I'd ever liked had started out like Quinn. Even Matt. Cute, popular, athletic. Typical. I couldn't help noticing Quinn—even though I wasn't trying to have anything to do with any boy at the moment.

"Well, if that's what you're after—then there you go," Jackson said, giving me a dismissive shrug and then going back to the dishes. "Quinn's a real winner, and so's his girlfriend."

"I'm not after anything," I said. "I'm just making pizza here."

"'Kay." He dried out the mixing bowl and handed it to me, but he wasn't smiling anymore.

Ms. Grady announced a quiz right then, so Jackson and I took our seats. I didn't get a chance to talk to him after that because we corrected the quizzes and then pulled the projects from the oven so they could be graded. We accepted our C and ate the funky-looking pizza, but we didn't chat.

I left the class feeling frustrated. I was just trying to make some lame pizza, not deal with some random boy-drama. *Give me simplicity,* I thought as I walked to the town library after school. *Simplicity and a cool, quiet field.*

The Rockville library was in a converted brick garage that used to belong to the volunteer fire department. It seemed like a kooky place to hang out and read, but there was a nice old guy working there who signed me up for my card and then pointed me in the direction of the fiction stacks. I had to do a book report on Hemingway's *A Farewell to Arms* and actually needed to read it. What I'd told Jackson hadn't been a total lie.

"Checking out something fun?" asked Melanie, rounding the corner of the periodical section, her arms full of glossy magazines.

I held up my book. "A classic," I said.

She gave me a funny look. "Yeah, I heard you pulled a *classic* today in Creative Living."

"What?"

"You know, I thought you were halfway cool, but Jane told me how you were flirting with my boyfriend." She paused. "You better stay away from Quinn."

My mouth dropped open. "Are you joking? We're not even friends—and he came and talked to me."

"Uh-huh. Jane saw it all. She told me everything."

Though Melanie didn't deserve an explanation, now I was mad. "Look, I have no interest at all in your boyfriend."

"Right."

"Whatever, I don't have time for this," I said, pushing past her. Her stack of magazines went crashing down in a messy pile all over the floor.

"Nice work!" she said.

I turned to help her clean up the mess.

"Leave it alone," she said.

"No, come on, let me help," I said, reaching for a *People*.

"Don't you get it? I don't need anything from you. No one in this town does." She walked off, teetering on her high-heeled sandals.

I clutched my book and went to check it out, blood still rushing in my ears. I didn't like confrontations—especially stupid ones over boys. It reminded me of the end of last spring when I'd begged Chelsea to leave Matt alone—only then, it had been for her safety, not because I'd loved him. Then again, if Chelsea and Matt hadn't hooked up, maybe he and I would have still been together.

It could have been much worse for me. Much, much worse.

Because I would have stayed with Matt, kept making excuses for the mean things he said to me, the ways he hurt me, and the way I felt about myself when I was with him. I'd have stayed there because I loved him. Now, though, I felt like that wasn't love at all. I couldn't tell you what it was. I was pretty sure that everything that had passed for love between me and Matt had been a lie.

And it still hurt.

I stood there in the parking lot, holding back tears and waiting for Aunt Mae's rusty pickup to rattle into the lot. All I could think about was escaping to the clearing.

A little while later, I helped Mae into the house with her grocery bags and dumped my backpack off on the couch.

"You're awfully quiet again, sweetie," Mae said, hanging up her coat. She hadn't said anything about my red face during the drive in from town, but now I braced myself for what was to come.

"Bad day?" she said, fishing.

"Yep."

Mae paused for a second, like she was waiting for me to tell her all about it, but I didn't say anything. "Well, how about a nice dinner?" she said, finally. "That should cheer you up."

"I'm going to go for a walk first. Is that okay?"

Mae nodded. "Certainly. A walk ought to clear your mind. I'll pop some chicken in to bake. I don't need much help. Oh, but you could bring in a head of cabbage for slaw on your way back."

"Okay." I slipped out the door, sucking in air like I hadn't breathed all day. I could smell the warm afternoon, the scent of dirt and grass rising up on the breeze.

Katie-dog trotted behind me, probably thinking we were going to play fetch. When I got to the clearing, though, Katie stopped and lay down under a tree, her watchful eyes on me the whole time. I gave her a last look as I faded into the mist.

"Henry?" I called into the fog. I reached the stump where we'd met the day before. There was no sign of Henry, his book, or his lawn mower. I felt a little sad, and I realized that maybe I hadn't been craving the stillness of the clearing as much as Henry's company.

"Hello?" I took a few more steps. The air felt thicker around me, filling all the spaces around my body like water in a pool. There was a low hum in my ears, electric-sounding, heavy.

"Henry?" I said again, my voice echoing in my ears. I took a few more steps. Ahead of me, where the mist began to fade, I could see a path, worn, freshly mowed. That had to be Henry's work.

I walked toward the path, and suddenly my vision blurred and the hum was louder again. Goose bumps prickled up and down my arms. I suddenly felt I should turn around.

But now, I didn't want to leave without saying hi. Even though I liked being with Aunt Mae, I wanted to talk to someone—a friend. Henry couldn't be too far from here. If he had been mowing a path near the clearing, his farm should be on the other side of it.

"Where are you?" I tried one last time, my voice weak-sounding against the electric hum. And then, dizzy, I took a few more steps forward, and the clearing broke away.

I was on the edge of somewhere else.

Bright hot summer sun surrounded me, and in the distance stood a classic white farmhouse that looked like it belonged in a painting. Laundry flapped on a clothesline. The sound of tinny big band music drifted on the breeze. An old man in a hat slept in a hammock strung between two fruit trees. A red, old-fashioned Ford truck gleamed like brand-new in the driveway.

And then I glimpsed Henry, running toward me as I fell to the ground.

CHAPTER SIX

What is she doing here? Henry barely caught Amy as she tumbled forward. He helped her down to the ground, aware of how light she felt in his arms, how she smelled like early fall—wood fires and ripe apples. Her eyes were closed and she had a scared look on her face, a look of uncertainty. Henry was scared, too.

Amy had crossed the clearing. Henry anxiously glanced over his shoulder toward the house. His grandfather still dozed in the hammock, and the curtains were drawn across his mother's second-floor bedroom window.

He stopped holding his breath and focused on Amy. "Are you feeling all right?"

Her eyelids fluttered open. "Henry," she said in a wheezy voice, "I was looking for you—and then I felt so weird. I'm wiped." She looked down at Henry's arms wrapped around her and seemed to stiffen, but she didn't pull away.

"Sorry. You were falling," he said. "I didn't want you to hurt yourself." Henry let her go and sat back on his heels.

Amy lowered herself to the grass and put her head between her knees. She was breathing heavily, still winded from the crossing.

A moment later, she raised her head. "Henry, why is it so hot all of a sudden? On the other side of the clearing—at my house—it was about to rain." She was doing it again—searching him up and down, studying his clothes and shoes.

Henry's heart beat faster. "Could still rain," he said nervously. "I always smell rain coming," he added.

"It's so pretty over here," she murmured, turning her attention to the farmhouse in the distance behind them. "And look at that classic truck—it's so shiny, it looks like new. You must have spent hours restoring it."

Henry cleared his throat. "It's like new, all right," he said. "Listen, let's take a walk."

Amy put her hands on her knees and forced herself up. "Yeah, that would be good." She took a step in the direction of the path to the house.

Henry placed a hand under Amy's elbow and steered her back toward the clearing.

"Oh. I thought you would show me around your farm," she said, stopping in her tracks.

"I promise I will—some other time, though," he said, instantly regretting the lie. He'd never show Amy around. He couldn't take the chance that bringing her across might change something. He couldn't take the chance that something awful might happen.

"Come along," he said, and they stepped into the misty clearing. Henry noticed Amy's movements were quick, fearful, as they entered the mist.

"There it is again," she said, shuddering. "The electric feel. It almost hurts." They went a little farther, and then she sank down onto the stump. "Don't you notice it? When I came through the mist on my side, I heard just the humming, but over on yours, the air was so heavy and buzzing and then I broke through and it was clear like a summer day. Man, I'm still dizzy. I feel like I'm going to faint."

"Wait here for a moment, please." Henry ran back to the house, giving Amy a look over his shoulder to make sure she'd stayed put. At the sink he pumped water into an empty jug, then grabbed a few other things and headed back to the clearing. He passed his grandfather snoring away in the hammock and the line of laundry flapping in the breeze.

Back inside the curtain of white fog he found Amy standing, watching his approach. He held out the jug to her. "Drink some water," he said. "It'll help your dizzy spell."

She took a swig and then stared down at the jug. "Your mom collects old stuff, huh?"

He blinked at her. "I beg your pardon?"

"You know, most people would have just brought me a bottle of water, not a jug that looks like it's a zillion years old."

"No one uses water jugs over at your place?"

"Are you kidding?" Amy raised her eyebrows at him. "They do make plastic ones these days." She held up the jug, inspecting it. "This must be an antique, right?"

Henry chewed his lower lip. "Well, yes, I suppose so." He took a deep breath, the feeling finally sinking in that Amy wasn't from his time. When she'd finished drinking, he took the jug from her and set it on the ground.

"Thanks again for the water, Henry. That's the nicest thing anyone's done for me all day." She seemed to study him again. "It's been a really crappy afternoon. You're so lucky you don't have to go to that stupid school."

"Is that why you were trying to find me? I heard you calling me . . . before you . . . came over to my side of the field." He didn't tell her he'd been loitering again near the edge of the clearing, waiting for her, hoping she'd come again to break his boredom.

Amy nodded and reached down to take another drink from the water jug. "You know the Hutchins family? They've got a flashy son and he's got an annoying girlfriend."

Henry had known the Hutchins family that lived over on Russell Road in his time. "Yep. I know of them."

"Then you know what a pain in the butt that kid's girlfriend is," Amy said. "I'm so . . . I don't know what."

"Angry. I think you mean angry," Henry said.

Amy bit her lip. "I just wanted to go away. Do you ever feel like that?"

"Yes. Often," he replied. "Not that there's anywhere to go." He looked off toward the east—the farthest he'd been in the clearing. "Well, maybe one place. I could show you one neat spot."

"Is it close by? Mae's cooking me dinner." She looked up at Henry, and he saw her face filled with an emotion he couldn't quite read. "I mean, maybe I shouldn't wander off." *With you.* That was the implied message in her eyes.

"Don't worry, it's only a stone's throw from here. We can leave at any time you decide."

"Okay," Amy said finally. "But just for a few minutes, then I gotta get back." She pointed at the bundle in his arms. "What's that stuff?"

"You'll see," he said. He led Amy down a short path through dense bushes and brambles. The curving trail emptied out onto a small patch of grass overlooking the creek. On the other side of the water was a curtain of white fog—the boundary of the clearing that Henry hadn't dared cross.

"Pretty," Amy said. "And more mist."

Henry set down the bundle he'd been carrying and unwrapped from it a wool blanket, which he shook out and spread on the ground.

"What are you doing?" Amy asked, her voice suddenly stiff, wooden.

"It's damp on the ground here."

Amy glanced back toward the path. "I, um, I don't know if—"

"Oh, geez," Henry said, blushing. "No, no. I'm a heel. Forgive me for giving you the wrong idea. I only wanted you to be able to sit awhile and watch the creek. You see, it'll help you take your mind off your troubles."

Amy crossed her arms and looked toward the path. "I should probably go back."

"You can trust me, Amy." Henry paused. "Look, I'll stand right here by the willow while you sit on the blanket. I promise."

Amy cautiously took a cross-legged seat on the blanket.

"I didn't mean to make you feel uncomfortable," Henry insisted, sensing Amy's fear hadn't subsided.

"It's okay," she said. "I get it. It's all right. You're not a jerk or anything." She stared down at the water bubbling over the rocks.

A dragonfly whirred past them and landed on a stone in the creek. Henry leaned back against the tree trunk, feeling its lumpy detail through his shirt.

"Yesiree. The creek is the most peaceful place I've found."

"You can sit down," Amy said, gesturing toward the other side of the blanket.

"No, that's fine," Henry said. "This willow is like an easy chair."

Amy allowed herself a small laugh. "You lie."

"No, I'm serious. And I wouldn't want you to think anything untoward was going on."

Amy shook her head. "Now you're just making fun of me," she said.

"No, I'm not. A boy spreads a blanket on the ground in a place—even a farm boy like me knows that old ploy. Except mine wasn't a ploy."

Amy sighed. "I didn't think you were like that, Henry. It's just . . . well, sit down, okay? And did I mention I have an attack German shepherd over at Mae's?"

"No, you didn't mention that." Henry sank down next to Amy on the blanket. "This is better than the willow tree; you were right."

Amy smiled and plucked some blades of grass, tossing them toward the creek. "Yeah."

"You still feeling dizzy?" Henry asked.

Amy turned her body to face him. "No."

"Are you still afraid of me?"

Amy laughed again. "Afraid of you? You're the most normal guy I've met in Rockville. I don't think I would have come out here with you if I'd felt otherwise."

"So you think I'm normal, huh? Is that a good trait?"

"Well, normal's not the right word. Most guys I've known, like you said, they'd have brought the blanket out for one thing and one thing only."

"Hmm, but would they have brought these?" Henry untied an embroidered linen napkin filled with biscuits. "Sorry I didn't swipe any jam for them."

"Snacks?" Amy's eyes lit up. "You brought us *snacks?*"

"These are left from dinner," Henry said. "Suppertime's a long ways off yet, and I was getting hungry. I figured you might be peckish, too."

Amy took a bite of one of the biscuits. "Holy crap, these are good."

"Holy *crap?*" Henry laughed at Amy's strange expression. "They're just Mom's everyday biscuits," he said, taking a healthy bite.

"Mmm, I think I would weigh a million pounds if I ate these every day," Amy said around a mouthful of biscuit. She laughed, wiping crumbs away with the sleeve of her jacket. "Sorry, I'm rude, talking with my mouth full."

Henry grinned and took another bite. He watched Amy's eyes brighten as another dragonfly whizzed by to land on some reeds at the edge of the creek. Her eyes looked brownish gold now in the soft sunlight, like the color of amber. Framed against the blue of the wool blanket and the green of the grass around them, they were stunning. He must have been staring, because Amy stopped in midbite.

"What?" she said. "You look funny."

Henry felt his cheeks get hot. "Sorry. I don't mean to stare."

Amy looked down at the biscuit in her hand.

"You're a real pretty girl, Amy. I don't mean anything by that, except to tell you so you know." Henry busied himself picking crumbs off the blanket so he didn't have to see Amy's reaction.

She touched his hand, stilling it on the blanket and covering it with her own. "That's a sweet thing to say." Amy's eyes looked glassy, on the edge of tears.

Henry's heart clenched inside his chest. *What did I do?* "I'm sorry," he said, pulling his hand from hers.

"For what?" Amy said. She wiped at her wet eyes.

"Sometimes I say things I should keep to myself," he said.

Amy chewed her lower lip. "No one really said that to me before—that I was pretty."

"No one?"

"No one who didn't want anything from me," she said in a quiet voice.

"Oh." It all made sense to Henry now. The blanket. How she's seemed scared to be back here alone with him. It wasn't just Amy being prim. Some creep had hurt her somehow. He let out a breath, trying to calm the anger building inside him. He wanted to ask Amy more, but it wasn't like him to pry. And truly, Amy didn't know him from Adam. He didn't have the right to ask her anything.

They sat there in silence, the sun shifting slightly overhead. Amy stayed in her cross-legged position, but after a while, Henry lay back on the blanket and searched the clouds for animal shapes. He felt like he could rest there forever, studying the heavens.

After Henry pointed out a few good cows and roosters overhead, Amy leaned back on her hands and looked up.

"Definitely a dragon," she said, pointing at a swirly collection of clouds to the east.

"Yes, now you've got the idea."

"It's not like I haven't done this before," Amy said, punching him on the arm. "It's just been a long while since I took the time."

Henry rubbed the newly sore spot. "Look over there—it's a mermaid."

"Good one."

"I see a volcano right over top of us," he said, after a moment.

"I don't see it," Amy replied.

"Lean back," Henry said.

Amy lowered herself back on her elbows. Tilting her head back, she let out a deep breath and seemed to relax. "Okay. Now I see it."

Henry was acutely aware of Amy's presence next to him on the blanket. His fingers itched to reach out and take her hand, but he didn't dare move.

Together they lay there, not talking. Minutes and more minutes went by, the only sound the rush of the creek and the breeze rustling through the willow's branches. It was like being in a cocoon, Henry thought. Being with Amy was peaceful, more peaceful than the creek, more peaceful than staring at the clouds. Just being with her, his new friend Amy.

At least, he *thought* they were friends now. He dreaded what might happen when he was forced to tell her about his situation. When Amy figured out why he wouldn't show her around his farm. When she discovered he was some kind of half person living a ghost's existence.

Because suddenly that was what Henry's summer felt like—a pale imitation of what once had felt so real.

Amy looked down at her left wrist and sat up. "My watch stopped. I probably should be getting back. I've been gone a long time." She jumped to her feet and shook crumbs and grass off her clothes. "What time is it?"

"I'm not sure, but I should get home to supper." Henry got up and folded the blanket, but Amy was already moving toward the path. "Wait—I'll walk you back," he called.

"I can walk myself. I'll be fine," Amy said over her shoulder.

Henry snatched up the blanket and what was left of the napkin of biscuits, then followed her down the path. She was far ahead, running now toward her edge of the clearing—all on her own. Henry felt his heart clench again, felt that Amy needed him. Walking back to the house, he realized he'd never worried like that over a girl before.

There was something about Amy, something that made him want to keep her from harm. Something that made him miss her seconds—or lifetimes—after she'd disappeared beyond the mist.

As Henry crossed back through the clearing, darkness was gathering. Darkness that seemed as sudden to Henry as the sound of crickets starting up their serenade. He had been with Amy longer than he'd thought.

"Where in blazes have you been, boy?" Grandpa called from the porch as he approached.

Henry bolted up the steps of the house to meet him. "I'm sorry. I was down at the creek and I lost track of time," he said. "Supper ready?"

His grandfather eyed him sternly. "Supper's come and gone. You're in the doghouse with your mother."

Henry's chest fell. He paused with his hand on the door handle. "I missed supper?"

His grandfather nodded and packed tobacco into his pipe.

This wasn't supposed to happen. Henry had lost track of the day, which he never let himself do. He'd forgotten that sometimes, the clearing had its own sense of time that didn't correspond to his regular day. He'd noticed it once before, when he'd fallen asleep reading near the stump, but this was much worse.

"Mother in the kitchen?" Henry asked.

"Bedroom." His grandfather's voice was icy.

The bedroom was not a good sign. The bedroom was where Mother retreated when she felt faint, or just wanted to sleep away the time. Normally, she only napped there, but Henry remembered previous days of this summer when she'd cried in her room for hours. She cried over Robert and his old letters from the spring, letters telling of training, and then letters from England as his unit prepared for the invasion. She cried over the loss of Henry's father in a logging accident up on Deer Mountain long, long ago. Crying was something Mother did a lot of.

"You best get in there and apologize," Grandpa said.

"Yes, sir." Henry went inside and mounted the stairs to the upper floor. He knocked lightly on his mother's door but didn't wait for a reply before opening it.

As he feared, Mother lay in the bed, her bottle of pills next to her on the night table. Henry's heart stilled. The guilt from his selfish, selfish moments down at the creek formed a pit in his stomach. He moved toward her swiftly.

"Mother, I'm here," he said, taking her hand.

Her eyes fluttered open, and Henry felt a sense of relief.

"I made a chicken fricassee," she said weakly.

"Yes, I'm terribly sorry. I lost track of time."

Mother glanced toward the night table.

Henry followed her gaze to the pills. "What's wrong, Mother? Are you feeling ill?" he said.

She sat up in bed against the pillows. "I need my medicine, son. Will you fetch me some more water."

"How many pills did you take this afternoon?"

She frowned at him, her pretty face taking on a tired, older look.

"Dr. Norris said those are only for your body aches," Henry said. "Did you already take a few pills?"

"I don't need a lecture on my health, thank you," she said, pulling up the blankets around her. "I would like you to bring me some water, please."

Henry shook his head. "Mother, there's no reason for you to feel bad on my account. I was rude to miss supper. I'm so very sorry."

"I was worried sick," Mother said, wearily.

"Yes, ma'am."

She closed her eyes. "I couldn't bear to think of something happening to you, Henry. Just couldn't imagine my dear, sweet boy not with me."

"Yes, but I'm fine. See? Everything is fine."

His mother's voice was hushed as she continued. "I was worried when your grandfather couldn't find you. He wandered the farm for a good hour searching. He was so worried."

Henry heard her fear building. "Say, let's go downstairs now, and you'll have your tea and I'll have a big piece of the cold chicken. I'm starving."

His mother reached out to clutch his hand again, squeezing too hard. "Don't you go away on me. I can't lose all my men."

Henry sucked in a breath. Yes, to his mother, even his being missing for a few hours added to the feeling of loss she carried with her. "Shall we go downstairs now?"

Mother finally loosed her grip on Henry's hand. "Be a dear and hand me my slippers."

Henry stood up from the bed and got them, along with her housecoat. Mother swung her legs over the side of the bed and slowly slid into her slippers. Once solid on her feet, she pulled the coat on over her nightdress.

And, Henry noticed, slid the bottle of pills into her pocket.

CHAPTER SEVEN

The woods were inky dark, but I wasn't scared. In fact, I almost felt a little cheerful. The time at the creek with Henry had been just what I needed. I skipped up the back steps to Mae's place and went into the house through the back door.

"I'm home," I yelled. The smell of baked chicken hung deliciously in the air. My stomach growled as I passed through the kitchen, where empty dishes sat on the table, waiting. But Mae was in the living room, watching TV from her recliner, a strange expression on her face.

"What's going on?" I said. "Not hungry?"

"I beg your pardon?" Mae said. She picked up the remote and muted the TV.

"I know I'm late for dinner. You didn't have to wait for me to eat," I said, plunking down onto the couch.

Mae gave me a look. "Amy—it's near ten o'clock."

I gaped at her. "Um, that's impossible. I was just out in the field and then down by the creek. It didn't seem that long."

"Sweetie, I was out there calling for you for the last two hours. I had half a mind to call the neighbors to gather a search party."

"I was just in the field."

Mae shook her head slowly, looking at me with pure disappointment.

I considered telling Mae about Henry, but then thought better of it. Even if she didn't know his family, she was the type who might call his parents and embarrass me and Henry both.

"Why on earth would you go out there to the field where no one could find you?"

"Just wanted to be alone."

"Well, that'd do it. I never go out that way where the darn fog covers the far meadow. If you want to walk the property, there's other ways round, down the side road that runs by the creek and the old homestead. Not through that mist. You gave me a good scare."

I held up a hand. "Mae, I said I'm sorry—I get it."

"You can't do that to an old woman like me," she continued. "We're in this together, you know. If you go running off, I get nervous."

"I won't do it again," I said.

The look on Mae's face was making me feel like crap. I thought she was done, but she kept going. "Didn't your mother ever hold you accountable for anything?"

I shoved my hands in my hoodie's pockets. "I guess."

"I'll take that as a no. And maybe that's how you got here, sweetie."

I bristled. "Um, what do you mean by that?"

Mae sighed and gave me a weary look. "I only mean that if your mother had set certain limits, then maybe—"

"Then maybe I wouldn't have hooked up with a jerk like Matt? Is that what you mean?" Hot tears stung my eyes. "Mae, seriously?"

She got out of her chair and lowered herself gingerly onto the couch next to me. "Now, Amy, hold on a minute. I didn't mean to sound like an ogre. That's my tired, old, grouchy body talking. I can't hike around like I used to. I'm beat from chasing after you."

My heart was still racing. "Mae. Will you answer me? Is that what you seriously mean? I thought you said Mom did the best she could."

Mae smoothed the throw draped over the arm of the couch. "I just mean, if I'd been your parent, I wouldn't have let you grow up like this."

"But you're not." My voice sounded cold, even to my own ears.

"No," Mae said. "I'm just your old great-aunt. But while you're here with me, you'll live by my—no—*our* rules. And rule number one is pretty simple—don't run off."

"I didn't run off. I wasn't paying attention to the time."

Mae gave me a sad look. "My dear, time is the one thing you should pay attention to. One day, you'll find there's never enough of it." She got up and shuffled off to bed, leaving me there on the couch.

The next day was a blur. It started with Mae barely talking to me over our breakfast of cold cereal, progressed through Jackson and Lori chatting like I wasn't at the lunch table, and went on to teachers looking right through me. I was beginning to feel like a ghost that no one could see.

But I almost didn't care.

I spent the hours daydreaming about the creek and Henry. Feeling the scratch of the wool blanket beneath my arms. Savoring the taste of the buttery biscuit melting in my mouth. Hearing the sound of the stream rushing over stones. When life could be as simple as that, who needed the rest of it?

On the bus, I leaned against the window, enjoying the view of green fields and farms we passed, marveling at the beautiful browns and grays of the rocky hills around us, the deep rusts of the cattle, the blue-green water of the Skagit as we drove over the bridge and up the highway.

Somewhere after the blueberry farm, Lori slid into the seat next to me. "It's really too bad we don't have any classes together," she said. "Are you going to try out for soccer?"

"Um, no. I'm not really a soccer person anymore." I didn't tell her I'd been into a few different sports back at my old school. That was part of the old me.

"Oh, okay then," she said in a bored voice. She turned away and pulled a lip gloss and a compact mirror out of her purse.

I realized I was doing that antisocial thing again. "I'll be yelling for you on the sidelines, though," I said, giving her a smile.

"Cool," Lori said. She capped the gloss and leaned over closer to me. "Listen, I don't know if you're even interested, but I was going to have some people over tonight."

"Tonight?"

"Yeah. It's Friday, remember? My folks are headed down to visit my sister in Tacoma. I've got the place to myself."

"Oh, gotcha. Well, um . . . who's going to be there?"

"I'm trying to keep it small," she said. "Just a few select friends." She tilted her head at me. "I know you're just getting to know everyone. But, if you want to, just show up tonight . . ."

The bus lurched to a stop and I grabbed my backpack.

"See ya," Lori called as I headed down the aisle to the door. She was trying to be nice to me, I guess. I didn't know if she even really wanted me to come to her party, and really, I didn't know if I'd be able to go. Mae was probably still mad about yesterday.

Yesterday.

I still didn't get how what seemed like minutes with Henry had turned into hours. It was just being in good company, I guessed. He made me feel comfortable and the time had just zipped by. I doubted a party at Lori's would be half as fun as that afternoon with Henry.

I figured I should go, though. At least put in an appearance. Maybe I could bring Henry with me to Lori's. Would that be weird—bringing a homeschooled guy with me? It sure would make things easier going with someone I knew would want to hang out and talk. I wasn't sure I could face a house party on my own.

Mae agreed to let me walk over to Lori's place early that night. I think she was overjoyed I actually had made friends with the girl. I gave Mae a hug goodbye, since things seemed better between us, and headed out the door just before sunset.

But before I left for Lori's, I went to get Henry. I called his name as I reached his side of the mist, and he came jogging toward me in the clearing.

"Hello, again. What are you doing here?" He was wearing basically the same outfit from the day before—work boots, brown pants, suspenders, a white shirt with the sleeves rolled up over his strong forearms. Man, he was solid.

"Hey." I returned his bright smile.

His face was tan, which made his blue, blue eyes stand out and his teeth look white as milk. "Well," he said, clearing his throat, "you're all gussied up this evening. What's the occasion?" He brushed a hand through his sandy blond hair to smooth it. I figured all my staring must have made him self-conscious, but I couldn't help it. How had I not noticed that Henry was super cute?

I laughed and wrinkled my nose at him. "I wouldn't call this gussied up."

"What do you mean? Look at you—you're shiny."

"It's called a scarf. It's just got a few sparkles." I tugged at the ends of the accessory that was draped over my plain white tee and black zip sweatshirt.

"No, *you* look shiny." He pointed at my lips and then sort of blushed.

"Oh." I shrugged. "Gloss with gold flecks. It's my going-out look."

"So you're going out on the town?"

"Nah, just to Lori's down the road. That's why I came out to get you. I wondered if you might want to go."

"Oh, I see." He rubbed a hand across his jaw line.

I bit my lip, waiting for Henry's answer. I mean, not that I cared. We were just friends, but still. "It's probably going to be lame," I said, starting to feel heat creeping into my cheeks. "You don't have to go."

"It's very kind of you to invite me," Henry said. "But, I'm sorry. I can't accompany you."

"Okay. I understand," I said quickly.

Henry took a step toward me. "Amy, I really would like to go with you."

"It's okay, you don't have to explain," I said, just wanting to run now.

"Wait a second," he said as he reached out for my hand. "Really. If I could, I would." His hand felt warm and dry, and feeling him touch me was strange, but not uncomfortable. I got the sudden urge to hug him.

"I just wanted to go . . . as friends," I said, easing away.

He shoved his hands in his pockets. "I wasn't expecting anything else."

I looked up at him. His eyes were focused on me intently, and there was genuine warmth there. I never used to believe it when people said that someone had kind eyes, but just then it made sense, because Henry had them.

"You go on and have fun," he said. "I'll see you here again. Will you come tomorrow?"

I nodded and walked off toward my side of the clearing.

I knew he was watching me. It felt good. And terrifying.

"Ohmigosh! Cute scarf!" Lori met me at her front door, pulling me inside, where a virtual mass of kids was churning like an ocean. Loud country music blasted from a stereo somewhere, barely covering the roar of conversations and laughter.

"Just a few friends?" I reached into my bag and pulled out a jar of strawberry preserves, which Mae had insisted I bring to Lori and her folks.

Lori shrugged and abandoned the jar on a bookshelf next to a mini-statue of a jumping trout. "It's a little bigger than I planned," she said, throwing up her hands. She steadied herself against the bookshelf and tugged at the back of her tights. She'd gone from jeans and T-shirt at school to a short black dress and wobbly high heels. And she was extra wobbly, from what I could tell.

"Yeah, it's packed. Are all these people your friends?"

Lori reached out and put her hands on my shoulders, pushing me into the mass of kids. "Booze in the kitchen," she shouted, melting into the crowd herself.

I stood there for a minute, getting jostled and feeling totally out of place. After the second elbow to my side from a wild dancer, I forced my way through the partygoers and found the kitchen. A girl I remembered seeing in my AP English class handed me a can of beer. I took it from her, but I didn't crack it open; I was too stunned by her completely chugging down the one she'd taken for herself. Laughing, she threw the empty can into the sink and then fell into the arms of a guy in a Rockville Roosters shirt who escorted her off toward the living room dance floor.

"Hi," I said to two girls snacking from a bowl of chips.

They mumbled greetings to me, then went back to their conversation.

I rolled the cold can back and forth in my hands, and thinking about how in the old days, I'd have Matt to talk to. Matt to ease my way through the crowd of people I didn't know. Matt to make everything seem normal, regular.

"Not your favorite brew?" Jackson nudged me.

"Oh, hey," I said. "No, um, I'm not much of a drinker." *Anymore*, I added silently.

"Me neither." Jackson saluted me with his red party cup. "Pop," he said. "I've got the car tonight and my mom would kill me if I were out drinking."

"Cool." I didn't really know what to say next, so I stared at the collection of state-shaped magnets on Lori's green refrigerator. Alaska and Kentucky were holding down a school lunch menu. Idaho anchored a shopping list.

Cat food
Peanut butter
Toilet paper
Cheese

"Okay, well . . ." Jackson turned to go.

"Wait," I said. "Um, so, how did you like that last essay question on the English test?"

"It was okay," he said.

"I hope I passed." I leaned back against the fridge.

Jackson took a sip from his red cup. "Just wait until the midquarter exam. She really kills on that one," he said, looking back over his shoulder.

"Are you, um, do you have to go or something?"

Just then, a brunette from our math class slid up next to him. "Hey, Jackson, I need another beer!" she whined, tugging on his sweatshirt.

He gave me a sheepish look.

"Please, help yourself," I said, stepping out of the way.

"Amy—look, I'll catch you later," Jackson said.

But I was already moving toward the back porch, which I could see was nearly deserted. I sat down on a wicker bench, next to a guy who was propped up against a post snoring. I hadn't always been a wallflower—and yet here I was mostly all alone on a stupid bench. From my perch, I could see Lori's sprawling back lawn, bordered by a woodlot of evergreens. A rusty swing set was highlighted by a motion sensor light that kept flipping on and off as kids wandered by. *Click. Hum. Click. Hum.*

My thumb rubbed the tab of the beer. It wasn't like the sweet drinks Matt sometimes whipped up for me at the parties we went to, but beer had sometimes done the trick then, too. Drink after drink, and then Matt would start to get different. And if I hadn't had too much to drink myself, I would see it coming. The glaze that took over his eyes. The slow smile that eased across his face.

"How are we doing over here?"

I looked up to see Quinn, and I felt a small sense of relief. At least there was one person I could talk to. Someone to jar me out of these stupid thoughts about Matt.

Quinn plunked down next to me, elbowing the snoring guy awake. The guy gave him an annoyed look, but rose from the bench and then stumbled off into the party.

"So," Quinn said, "where were we? Oh, I know—how are we doing over here? And that's the part you fill in . . ."

"I'm fine," I said.

He set down the cup he was holding and took the beer from my hands. "See, you have to flip back this little tab." He gave me a slow smile as he handed back the open can. "Now you'll be more than fine."

"Yeah, thanks." I took it from him but didn't take a sip.

"Lori's folks are going to be so pissed when they get back from Tacoma tomorrow." He shook his head and swirled the drink in his hand.

"She doesn't normally party like this?"

"Not since I've known her." Quinn said. "But she invited Jane, who invited Melanie, and Melanie invited some friends, and so on, and so on." He took a long sip from his cup. "So where's Jackson?"

"How should I know?"

"Come on, the guy is drooling over you," Quinn said with a laugh. "Don't play that you don't see it."

"Jackson's here with some brunette from our math class," I said.

"Shelli Wilson," Quinn said, nodding. "That makes sense. They used to go out."

I shrugged. "Then I guess it does make sense." I set down the beer can and picked up a pillow embroidered with HOME, SWEET HOME. Jackson with his drunk ex, that was just great.

Quinn stroked back his long bangs and leaned against the post. "You know, it's pretty loud, even out here. We could go somewhere else to talk, if you want."

"Um, that's okay; this is fine."

"Well, I didn't mean just talk," Quinn said, his eyes twinkling.

I frowned at him. "Um, what about Melanie?"

"We're—we're not that serious," he said. "She doesn't know everything I do. I just figured you might like to get to know me better." Quinn scooted closer to me on the bench. "I don't know . . . There's something between us. Can't you feel it?"

I felt myself blush. I couldn't help it. I did think Quinn was cute—I had from the first time I saw him in the grocery store—but come on!

"Amy," Quinn whispered, his beer-scented breath fanning against my cheek, "you know it would be fun."

I sat very still for a moment, totally creeped out. I guess I hadn't thought that Quinn was like the random-hook-up party guy he seemed to be at the moment. I'd given him way more credit than he'd deserved. I stood up and said, "I've got to go."

"Don't run away." Quinn grinned, reaching out toward my hip.

I shoved the beer can into his open hand. "Later."

There was no reason to stay, so I walked back inside to thank Lori for inviting me. But no one I asked seemed to know where she was. That made me nervous. Even though I barely knew the girl, she'd seemed pretty smashed. I didn't like the thought of Lori passed out somewhere.

I pushed my way up through the crowd on the stairs and opened the first door. The room was empty except for a pile of coats and a white cat peeking out from under the bed.

The next door I pushed open was a bathroom, where a girl fixed her makeup at the mirror while another girl puked in the toilet.

"Sorry." I shut the door. "Lori?" I called as I went into the next room.

But it wasn't Lori. It was a couple sitting on a bed in the dark: Jackson and Shelli. I turned to go.

"Hey!" Jackson said. "Wait, Amy." He got up and walked to the doorway.

"No, it's okay. I'm just looking for Lori," I said. "Sorry."

"Is everything all right?" he asked.

"Yeah. It's fine. Totally fine. I'm heading out."

He put a hand on my arm. "You need a ride home or something?"

"No, I just wanted to find Lori."

"I saw her out on the front porch a little while ago."

"She seemed pretty wasted before."

"I'll keep an eye on her, I promise," he said. "I'll be right down to find her."

I glanced past his shoulder. Shelli was lying back on the bed now, knees up and hands flopped down at her sides.

Jackson noticed my stare. "Shelli's fine, too. I'll take her down to get some air."

"You guys sure know how to party," I said, leaning against the doorway.

He shrugged. "Some people get a little out of control. Don't tell me you guys didn't party in Seattle."

"No. We partied." I let out a breath I'd been holding.

"I promise nothing bad's gonna happen. I'll make sure of it."

I left Jackson in the doorway and headed back down the stairs. Forcing my way through the crowd, I felt more alone than ever, even though I was surrounded by more people than I had been in weeks. Outside, I finally found Lori on the steps, blowing a lop-sided smoke ring into the bluish-tinged glow of the porch light. Her eyes were half closed, but she was sitting upright. I didn't know if I could trust Jackson when he'd said he'd look out for her. I stood there thinking I should stay, but it was all too much.

All too familiar.

I sucked in clean, clear air as I jogged off down the driveway, grateful for the cover of the dark night.

The weekend passed slowly, and the rain came, dripping from the trailer's downspout into puddles outside my window. I lay in my bed, thinking of the night before and of the things I'd left behind. Getting used to Rockville was harder than I thought it would be. It didn't really seem like anyone was even halfway cool. Well, no one but Henry. I could have gone to see him, but after his weirdness about coming to the party, maybe he wasn't into hanging with me.

Several times, stupid as it felt, I punched the familiar numbers into my new cell phone—first Chelsea, then Matt—but I didn't hit Send. It was weird how even though they'd been such jerks to me, a part of me missed them, missed the easiness of being with them. I guess I just felt homesick. Or, maybe the same old stuff was easier to do than making something new.

Around four on Sunday, Mae knocked on my door, and then came in since I was zoning out to music and finishing up reading the Hemingway book for my report.

"Amy?" she mouthed.

I pulled out my earbuds.

"We have company," she said.

"Oh, okay." I followed her out into the living room, my heart pitter-pattering because I thought it was going to be Henry. Instead, I found Mom and Pete. I glanced from them to Aunt Mae, who was smiling, though it was strained. Instantly, I suspected she'd called them because of the other night.

"Hi, Ames," Mom said. She was wearing one of her typical weekend outfits—black yoga pants with a bright green track jacket. Her hair had new blond highlights and made her look even younger than she already did. She'd had me when she was barely out of high school and was way younger than the other mothers on our old block.

She came over and gave me a hug, while Pete just waved from his seat on the couch. "How was your first week at school?" she asked, releasing me.

"Fine."

"You folks chat, and I'll go put on some coffee," said Mae as if she hadn't expected Mom and Pete, which was hilarious since she'd probably known they were coming.

"Did Mae ask you to stop by?"

Mom looked confused. "We'd planned to take a drive up here once you settled in."

"And I've never seen the place," added Pete with a dry chuckle. "It's pretty, uh, rustic." He studied the living room, his gaze passing over the wood stove, the sloppy pile of kindling next to it, the bark bits on the floor, the marked-up linoleum, and peeling wallpaper in the dining room.

I felt a twinge of defensiveness. "It's comfortable. Mae keeps this place pretty nice."

"Of course," Pete said, coloring slightly. "I didn't mean anything by that."

Mom gave me a sharp look and then sat down next to Pete on the couch. She patted his leg. "Mae's made this her home for years, honey."

"I guess I pictured it more like a cabin," Pete said, clearing his throat.

"It's fine." I plopped down on the other end of the couch. "Lots of people live in trailers up here."

"Yeah," Pete said. He ran a hand through his thinning salt-and-pepper hair and then slipped an arm around Mom. "You're right."

"So, school?" Mom asked. "It's going okay? You're making friends?"

"Same old, same old."

"You like your teachers?"

"They're fine."

Humming, Mae shuffled in with a tray of steaming mugs and cream and sugar. I cleared some of the gardening magazines and newspapers from the coffee table, and she set it all down.

"Thank you, sweetie," said Mae. She distributed the mugs to everyone and then sat in her recliner.

"We didn't mean to spring a visit on you," Pete said. "We just wanted to make sure everything was going well for you two."

I sipped the hot coffee. Since I was already five foot eight at eleven years old, Mom had long ago realized coffee wasn't going to stunt my growth.

"I'm sorry, Mae, but I can't believe you called them to check up on me," I said.

"I didn't call them," she said.

"Okay . . ." I shrugged and took another sip of coffee.

"We wanted to check on you," Mom said, setting down her mug. "I didn't, well, I didn't feel right about the way we just shipped you off."

"I chose to come here; it's not like you abandoned me."

"I wanted to make sure you're really okay." Mom's green eyes looked watery.

"I'm okay. Why are you getting all weird?"

Mom shifted on the couch. "Well, here's the real reason we're visiting. With you and Pete's kids gone, we've decided to move. Pete's been offered a job in Phoenix, and I'd really love to live down there in the sunshine. I could use a change."

"What?" I nearly choked on my coffee. "You're leaving?" I didn't add *me. You're leaving me.*

"Nothing's finalized yet," Pete said. "A position's come up at another branch of my company. It's a nice promotion."

"I think he should take it," Mom said. "After all, you seem to be getting along well here with Mae."

I nodded robotically. Yes, things were going fine, but if Mom left, then that meant this was *it*. Mae's was going to be my only home.

"Now, is this something you have to decide on right away?" asked Mae. She glanced from Pete to me, concern in her eyes.

"Yes, unfortunately, it'd mean packing up in the next month or so. We'd be gone before December."

"Before Christmas," I murmured.

"Well, you and Mae could fly down for the holidays, of course."

Mae waved a hand. "I don't fly, and neither does Katie-dog."

I stirred more sugar into my coffee. "Whatever. The Holidays are no big deal, anyway." The pit in my stomach said otherwise. No Holidays. No family. No home. Nowhere to go back to in Seattle. Only here.

Mae reached out from the recliner and patted my hand. "This is quite a shock for the both of us, sweetie," she said.

"You can say that again," I muttered.

"Now wait a second, Amy. This is what you wanted, right?" Mom asked me.

"Well, yeah, but—"

"You wanted a change. You wanted to move up here."

"Yeah, I guess."

"Let me think of the exact words you used—'a life away from the old one.'"

"Yes." *But I didn't want a life away from her.*

"Well, isn't it turning out how you wanted?"

"It's fine."

Mom took a sip of coffee, and then moved on to other topics. They stayed awhile longer, chatting with Mae and me, though after that bombshell, there was nothing more I wanted to say. I stared out at the rain, realizing that I was here for good.

It made me want to run. And there was only one place to run to.

CHAPTER EIGHT

"Henry?"

He looked up from pea picking to see Amy standing there, her face pale, her arms wrapped around herself. Abandoning his bucket in the dirt, he ran to her.

"What are you doing over here?"

She shakily reached out to him, touching his sleeve as if she were trying to bring him closer to her. "Sorry, I didn't know where to go. I didn't know who else to talk to."

Henry wiped his hands on his trousers and then put a hand under Amy's elbow, walking her into the shade of one of the apple trees, out of view of the front of the house. She was weak from crossing the clearing, and she leaned into him, letting him guide her. He drew her under the broad branches, the sweet smell of the tiny apples swirling in the breeze.

He wasn't sure what had happened to make Amy so sad, but he was distracted by her nearness. Her lovely brown hair gleamed in the dappled sunlight, her lips were light pink like the apple blossoms that had fallen away in late spring. She was a picture he wanted to remember always. Henry was nervous, though, knowing that at any moment his grandfather could come around the corner, or his mother would leave her chair on the front porch and shatter the perfect moment.

"Amy," he said, sobering himself, "look, you shouldn't have come. It's not—" He saw her eyes fill with confusion, hurt, something. "No, please don't—I didn't mean . . . oh, gosh . . ."

Her lower lip quivered. "What? Do you want me to go?"

"Forgive me. Listen, nothing makes me happier than to see you." Henry fished a handkerchief from his pocket and held it out to her. "Tell me what's the matter."

Amy took the handkerchief from him, turned it over in her hands, and traced the letter H embroidered in white on white. "Thanks," she said, then dabbed at her wet eyes.

"You're welcome. Now will you please tell me what's happened?"

"My mom is moving away. She's leaving me and this place sucks and now there's nowhere to go. Nowhere to go." Her voice was quiet, trailing off as if she were embarrassed.

"So you came here."

"Yeah." She looked up at him, her eyes watery again. He couldn't help it; he circled his arms around her small body. She was stiff against him for a moment, but then with a large exhale, she relaxed against this chest.

"There now," he whispered. "Everything will be all right."

Unconsciously, Henry dipped his chin toward her hair and caught the fruitlike scent of her shampoo. Then, noticing what he was doing, he lifted his head again. He needed to be a gentleman, to remember that Amy had come to him for reassurance. But he couldn't let go, couldn't force his arms to release her, couldn't relinquish the feel of her so close.

After a moment, she pulled back, tears still dotting her eyelashes. "Sorry. I didn't mean to cry all over your shirt."

"It'll wash," he said. He reluctantly let go of Amy, but she barely moved, and that pleased him.

"Sorry." She dabbed at her eyes again and then balled the handkerchief in her fist. "I'm a mess. I just didn't know where to go."

"Amy, I—look, you can't come here again. Not here by the farm."

Her cheeks flushed red. "I don't understand."

"We need to go to the clearing now."

"Why? It's so much nicer over here at your place. It's raining at my house, but it's always sunny over here. I mean, it's like freaking *summer*..." She took a step back from Henry and crossed her arms. "Uh, why are there still baby apples on the tree here when our apples are all ripe or rotting?"

Henry didn't answer, but he took Amy by the hand. Hesitantly it seemed, she let him lead her, until at last they stepped into the clearing's cool blanket of white. Henry allowed himself a deep breath. "There, that's better." He made a place for her on the stump.

Amy still looked confused. "Henry, this is weird. I mean, the sun and the apple tree . . . and now you don't want me over there. I just wanted to go sit on the porch and talk."

Henry shook his head. "I'm sorry; that's impossible."

Amy frowned. "Why?"

"It's for a good reason. You have to trust me."

"You're kidding, right?" she said, standing up. "I live in a freaking trailer with my old aunt. How bad could your place be? It looks pretty sweet from what I've seen."

"It's difficult to explain," Henry said quickly.

Amy let out a laugh. "Come on, Henry. Seriously? You're hilarious," she said, taking a few steps back. A smile played on Amy's lips. The confusion and fear from before were gone. "I don't know what you think you're hiding."

"Now, hold on just a second," Henry said. He got up from the stump and followed her slow steps. She took one and then another toward the farmhouse side of the clearing. He sensed she would break into a run at any moment. "Stay put."

"Yeah, right." Amy winked at him.

"Now, don't do anything rash," he warned.

"Just try and stop me!" she said, laughing.

And then she did it—she ran toward the farmhouse, bursting through the heavy air and tumbling out into Henry's homestead ahead of him. She yelped as she jumped onto the grass. Henry's heartbeat stuttered in his chest. Terrified that someone would hear, he looked toward the backyard, but he didn't see his grand-father.

And then, Amy was on her feet again, far out in front of him, turning to see how far behind he was and laughing as she ran down the path to the house. Boy, she was fast. Henry caught up with her as she reached the front steps. But he didn't need to stop her.

She was stuck in her tracks, staring at the porch where Mother sat, eyes closed, in her rocking chair.

In her blue housedress with the red and white flowered apron, Mother looked pale as always. The news report was ending and or-chestra music drifted from the wireless in the living room. Mother rocked in time to the music, a wistful smile on her lips. Amy was frozen in place, watching her.

And Henry was frozen—watching Amy's strange expression and praying that his mother was not going to open her eyes while they stood there. After a moment of stillness, Henry reached for Amy's hand, breaking the trance.

"Please . . . follow me," he whispered.

When they got to the path and were out of sight of the porch, she said, "Your mom, she looks old-fashioned, too." Amy's face was colorless. "And the man on the radio sounded all crackly. Before the music, he was talking about the war. About the USO dance in Seattle. About the bombing in Germany."

Henry nodded.

"We're not at war with Germany," Amy said. "There hasn't been a war there since the 1940s. That was, like, eons ago."

Henry nodded again. "Yes, we're at war. My brother Robert . . . he's . . . he's over there."

"What's going on here?" Amy crossed her arms over her chest and glanced back at the farmhouse, at the shiny truck in the driveway. "That's a new truck, isn't it? That's not a classic."

"Yes."

"And the apple tree—and the summer days . . ." Amy's eyes clouded with emotion.

"Well—" Henry began.

"Great," Amy muttered, on the edge of tears. "Just great. If you're a ghost, then why can I touch you?" She punched his arm.

"Cut it out. I'm not a ghost."

"Uh-huh." Fear dawned on Amy's face as she stepped away from him, as if she were seeking distance for protection.

"Amy, let me explain. There's no reason to be afraid."

"You're not from here," she murmured.

"Yes, I am."

"No. No. It can't be. This isn't possible." Amy backed away from him, backed all the way through the empty field, watching him while she vanished into the mist like a ghost.

CHAPTER NINE

Running never seemed so right. My lungs burning, I broke through the mist, ignoring the buzzing around me as I charged out into the field. I fought my way through the woodlot until I was in sight of the house, and Katie, barking up a storm, came loping out to greet me and accompany me on my escape run.

I collapsed onto the back porch, sucking wind. The air was crisp, cool, and smelled of the fire in the wood stove. I could feel the wet AstroTurf-carpeted stairs beneath me and could hear Katie lapping from her water bowl. Yet nothing seemed real or concrete. I put my head between my knees. There was something weird about the clearing, all right. Either I'd been hallucinating, or I'd just had a run-in with freaking ghosts. There was no other explanation.

An incredible sadness filled me for the loss of the friend Henry could have been for me. But wait a second—I'd *felt* him. I'd punched him on the arm, and he was as real as anything. He'd fed me at the creek. And I'd hugged him.

No—he'd *held* me. I'd smelled the soap and sweat on his skin. I'd heard his heart beating. But he wasn't real. He didn't exist. He was a ghost.

While I didn't even believe in ghosts in the traditional sense, I did believe in the other kind, those people you couldn't let go. Those feelings that haunt you until you feel like you're living something over and over. Those ghosts I knew were real. But I wasn't so sure about a ghost who'd held me in his arms. A ghost who'd given me his handkerchief. *Wait.*

My heart pounding, I reached into my pocket and pulled out the balled-up hankie. There it was—the embroidered cloth Henry had given me, still wet with my tears.

The back door swung open. "Sweetie, what on earth are you doin' out here?" Mae said. "It's nearly time for dinner. I was about to send out another search party." She let Katie into the trailer.

I didn't move. "Do you believe in the afterlife?" I asked.

Mae stepped out onto the porch and plunked down into one of the chairs. "Well," she said with a tired laugh, "that explains it—you're out here thinking about life's big questions."

"No. I mean, well, kinda," I said. Mae was gonna think I was nuts if I went too far down this road, and I didn't want to be any trouble to her. "But for real, do you believe there's life after death?"

"I believe in heaven." She patted the chair next to her.

"But do you believe that people hang around after they die?"

"Like ghosts?"

"Yeah." I stuffed the handkerchief back in my pocket and took a seat by Mae.

"Well," Mae said, her brow wrinkled, "sometimes I miss the ones I loved who've passed on, and I think I feel their presence."

"Are they friendly?"

"Well, yes, of course." Mae laughed. "They're my loved ones, after all. Though I guess you can watch all kinds of ghost shows that claim unfriendly spirits are real, too. What happened on your walk to bring all this up? You think you saw a ghost?"

"I don't know what I saw."

"Well, this'd be a good valley for a haunting. There have been all kinds of strange things reported out here. Old haunted mining camps up at Crystal Creek. An occasional Bigfoot sighting."

"How about haunted houses?"

"I think haunted houses are *sad,* not haunted. When a house is abandoned, it loses its good feelings. Without people, it's got no love. Used to be a few abandoned houses around here. When my daddy bought this property and its run-down farmhouse, every-one swore it was haunted."

Goose bumps prickled my skin. "A farmhouse? What hap-pened to the people who lived there?"

"Not too sure," Mae said. "Just up and left their homestead, and their relatives sold off the property to my daddy. We moved in to that sad house, but it burned down a few years later. My mom and daddy moved back to the city for work, and I moved this trailer onto this end of the property eventually."

"This end of the property? Where was the house?"

"Down the road to the west. That's the only way to get to it. Otherwise, you run into fog and trees. It's just empty land now, but if you walk down the road, you can still see the homestead's old chimney bricks stacked in a heap."

"What if the ghosts from that haunted house stayed?"

"Ghosts only stay if you let them." Mae sighed. "I don't pre-tend to have all the answers, sweetie. But I think you've had bigger troubles than ghosts, so don't worry yourself about it."

"Right." I nodded.

"Now let's go inside and make some popcorn," Mae said, eas-ing out of her chair.

I followed Mae inside, but not without another glance toward the clearing. *Goodbye, Henry. Goodbye, ghost boy from the past.*

"The indirect object would be . . . ?" Ms. Mills paused by my desk.

Everyone paged through their English text, looking for the answer. I raised my hand, bored by the lesson as much as the Monday unfolding in front of me. "It's the suitcase," I said.

The bell rang and books slammed closed.

"Yes. Good, Amy. See you tomorrow, class."

Jackson walked over to my desk, shouldering his backpack. "You're quite the grammar queen," he said.

"Yeah." I shoved my stuff in my bag and we walked out into the packed hallway.

"You doin' okay, Amy?" Jackson asked. "You seem off today."

Off. Now that was a word. There were ghosts in the back of Aunt Mae's property. I was haunted by the kindest boy I'd ever met. He'd brought me biscuits, held me, and offered me his handkerchief. And it was all unreal. I had to be sick or something—maybe crazy.

"Amy?" Jackson tugged at my hand. "Space-case? Are you all right?"

"Yeah, I'm fine." I headed out the door, but Jackson was on my heels.

"Did you have fun at Lori's party?"

"I think you had more fun than I did," I said, giving him a pointed look.

"Yeah, it was a good thing you had me check on Lori—she passed out about a half hour after you left."

I nodded. "Well, I'm glad you were there." I spun my combination and threw open the door of my locker. Jackson stood there, looking like he had more to say.

"Yeah?" I said.

"Oh, I was going to ask if you wanted to—"

I stiffened.

"Be on the homecoming committee," Jackson said slowly. "You okay? You look like I just asked you to join a cult."

"No, no," I said. I had to remember that Jackson was cool. He was just a friend and not some guy after me. "Sorry. Yeah, homecoming committee, sounds like a load of fun."

He shrugged. "I know it's kinda lame, but being involved in school activities always helps for scholarship applications. Anyway, I volunteered to co-chair it with Lori. If we leave it to the same old people, it'll suck as usual."

"What? Who?" As we walked, I stopped to wave at Lori, who was all the way down the hall.

"The same old people," Jackson continued. "You know, Melanie and her crowd. You should have seen her face when Mr. Planter announced me and Lori as co-chairs in leadership class." We stopped by his locker.

"I never knew a guy who cared about homecoming."

He gave me a hurt look and opened his locker. "Thanks."

"I didn't mean that the way it sounded."

"I know," he said. "But I'm not Mr. Football. And I'm more organized than most of those airheads, anyway." He threw his English book into his locker and grabbed his physics and calculus texts.

"Um, well—"

"Seriously, Amy," he said, shutting the locker with a bang, "you don't have to do it. I just thought it might be fun and that you could meet some people. I mean besides the ones at Lori's lame party."

I felt like a jerk. "Well, I guess I'll think about it."

"Really?"

I noticed how blue-green Jackson's eyes were, how they were rimmed with navy and the centers were golden. Had I never even noticed the color of his eyes before?

In my silence, he turned to leave.

I grabbed his arm. "Wait. I appreciate this, Jackson. You're trying to help me get involved. I get it. I'm just not used to people being so nice to me."

"Your friends should be nice," Jackson said. "Isn't that why you're friends with them?"

"I've never had guy friends," I admitted.

Jackson raised an eyebrow. "Maybe that's the problem."

"I mean, I had a boyfriend, but I didn't have someone I could count on."

"You couldn't count on your boyfriend?"

I felt small and weak in the hallway, and suddenly aware of the crush of people around us, of the smell of half-finished lunches and mint gum, of cologne covering gym sweat and nervousness. "No, I couldn't count on him. Or on anyone."

"That stinks," Jackson said.

I couldn't help but giggle at the word. "Yeah, it stinks all right."

"Well, I'm just talking about the homecoming committee. Nothing major—not brain surgery. So what do you say?"

"Sure," I said. The bell rang and we moved down the hall.

Jackson paused before peeling off toward physics. "And just for the record, you can count on me," he said.

I nodded at Jackson, feeling that he meant well—and that he probably was a good guy. Maybe, since the only other friend I'd made wasn't even real, I should give him a chance. "Thanks," I said.

Jackson smiled and walked away down the hall. I swear he seemed to walk a little taller. I wasn't sure what to make of that.

CHAPTER TEN

It was two days later, two days of Henry waking to a bright morning. And then his waking blended with the farm chores, and the mowing, the sleeping in the hammock, and the same old conversations with his mother and grandfather: *Yes, the haying would be busy at the end of summer. Yes, the apple trees were thick with fruit this year. No, it didn't smell like rain.* And it never did. Day after day, the sun hung overhead, as gold as a fresh egg yolk.

Besides the sun, though, there was a newer constant of this particular summer—Amy. Or at least there had been. Since Henry had met her, she came to his mind often, as much a fixture of his world as anything else. And she hadn't been to see him since the other day. He knew he'd scared her off.

He had half a mind to cross the clearing—just to peek over into Amy's place—but the familiar fear returned to his stomach. He could imagine all this disappearing, vanishing because he didn't want to preserve it badly enough anymore. Henry didn't want to think about what would become of his mother.

But, boy, he missed Amy.

He rocked on the back porch, recalling the delight on her face as she'd finally relaxed at the creek and had let herself see the shapes in the clouds. He got the feeling that she didn't let herself relax very often. The guardedness in her eyes haunted him. Deep brown eyes, framed by sparkly eye powder and something deeper, something painful that shaded them from within, and yet made them all the more beautiful.

"You out here dreaming again?" Grandfather's voice cut into his reverie.

"No, sir." Henry sat up, drawn instantly into the bright, bright summer day in front of him.

Grandfather shook his head. "We have work to do before your mother calls us for dinner."

"Yes, sir."

The old man turned to go, muttering to himself.

"Grandpa?" Henry followed him down the steps. "What about a game of checkers?"

"Why, I haven't the time for that foolishness at the moment," the old man answered, with a wave of his hand.

"Just one game," Henry said. Even if he did know all of Grandpa's moves, checkers was one way to pass the time and, hopefully, not think of Amy.

"Tonight after supper, perhaps," Grandpa said. "Not now. We've got more peas to pick."

"Yes, sir."

Henry walked out into the garden, through the rows and rows of trellised peas, but his eyes were on the path to the clearing. He picked bushel after bushel of the pods. He picked until his hands were dirty and sticky and the sun was high, and then he turned to weeding the potato hills. He put off the mowing, unable to stand the idea of being disappointed by Amy's not coming to see him. When the call came for dinner, he was glad.

After the ham, potato salad, and fresh greens, Henry was nearly stuffed. He forced himself to lift a last bite of leftover birthday cake to his mouth. Vanilla icebox melted on his tongue, the fluffy frosting light and sweet—cloyingly sweet.

"Those were some good groceries," Grandpa said with a nod to Mother. "And now, if you'll please excuse me, folks, the porch is calling."

"Thank you, Mother. That dinner was fine," Henry said, breaking the silence that fell at the table.

Mother studied Henry, taking a sip of tea and leaning back in her chair. She gave him an encouraging smile. "Are you going to tell me, son? Who was she?"

Henry dropped his fork. It glanced off his plate and clattered to the ground. He fumbled for it. "What do you mean?"

"The girl with you the other day in the yard. Strange girl. I was half asleep in my chair. Thought she was a dream at first. I meant to ask you, but it slipped my mind."

Henry stared down at his plate. It was the everyday china, the set with blue flowers. He studied the intricate petals, the twining greenery. His mind raced as he realized that not only had Mother seen Amy—she'd also remembered her.

"Beautiful little gal," his mother continued. "Is she visiting family here?"

Of course Mother would ask that. All of her life she'd lived here in the valley, and for people like Mother, the world started and ended in these Cascade foothills, at the river's headwaters. Here in the valley they had everything they needed. It was a world unto itself.

People talked the same, cooked the same food, lived the same hard-working lives. To them, there was nothing outside the valley, and no reason for an outsider to appear, other than to visit a relative. And that was how Henry had thought, too—until Amy.

"She's a new girl," he said, not wanting to lie to his mother.

Her forehead wrinkled and her blue eyes widened with interest. "She's staying with kin up here? Do we know them, son?"

He shook his head. "Moved up with her aunt," he said, "but she's new around here, too." He touched his napkin to his lips and then set it next to his empty plate.

"You know, son, the poor dear could use some new clothes," his mother said. "Maybe the pastor's wife and I could put together a basket of things for the family next Sunday."

Henry tried not to show alarm. "No, no. That's an awfully

nice thought, Mother, but it's not necessary," he said in a gentle voice.

"Well, a girl that pretty can't go through life looking like a ragamuffin."

Henry just nodded.

"Will you tell me why you didn't ask her to stay for supper?" she said. She poured herself another cup of tea and reached for the honey jar. "Thought I raised you better than that, Henry."

"Mother, she couldn't stay. She's shy, anyway."

"I only meant it would be nice for you to have a friend's company, son."

"I just saw Leon when school let out," he said, wincing with the memory of his long-lost best friend. Long lost because school was a lifetime ago. He knew he wouldn't see Leon again.

"Well, perhaps I meant a young lady friend," his mother said, adding a little smile. "It's been a while since we've seen you with anyone."

Henry's cheeks pinked up. He'd been pretty popular with the girls at school, never been at a loss when it came to finding a date to the dances. The girls at school, though, had seemed too preoccupied with dreaming up their future lives together. The last girl he'd liked—Margaret Hillman—had filled pages of her science notebook writing "Mrs. Henry Briggs" over and over, but hadn't been much fun to talk with. Henry didn't miss the companionship of those girls. He hadn't thought about them in ages.

But Amy was a different matter. What he wouldn't give to see her again.

"She seemed like a nice girl," Mother continued. "You should bring her round again. Maybe she's just the girl for you."

Henry smoothed the napkin on the table and was tempted to refold it. "Mother, I'm afraid that's not possible."

"You never know," she replied, taking a sip of tea.

"No offense, Mother, but this time I do know. She's not for me," he said. "She's from far, far away."

His mother's blue eyes filled with concern. "You must really be sweet on her," she said after a moment. "You've never been bashful about bringing a gal around the farm before."

"Yes, I do like her," Henry said, "but she won't be back to see us."

Mother set down her teacup. "Why on earth not?"

"Half the town's gone to war or down in the shipyards. The mill's running at full capacity. No one's coming around visiting, Mother."

"She was here. Don't tell me no one's coming round."

Henry felt a tingling feeling in his bones, as if this were the moment when Mother would finally understand what they were living. The moment when she'd grasp the situation and he wouldn't be alone with the truth anymore. "She's not supposed to be here, Mother. She's from the future."

Mother nodded, her face drawn. "Yes, of course, how foolish of me not to notice," she said in a tired voice.

"I am telling you the truth. Why won't you believe me?" Exasperation seized Henry. He spoke very slowly. Deliberately. "Every day is summer. Every day, Mother. Haven't you noticed? Aren't you awake? Can't you see what's going on here? Don't you miss the fall—or winter? We haven't seen rain or snow in ages."

"I see you've been reading those science fiction comic books again."

Henry knew it was pointless to keep going, but the frustration in him welled beyond control. "That girl you saw doesn't exist yet. I told you—she is living in the future. That is why she can't come to dinner with us, because if she does, maybe all of this would collapse!"

Mother's mouth was set in a hard line, her eyes filling with tears. "Henry, I've never known you to tell me such rubbish. What has got into you? Why would you say these strange things to me?"

Henry's stomach felt queasy. He steadied himself against the chair. "Yes, Mother. I know it sounds crazy." He paused, letting the wave of emotion leave him. He saw the confusion and hurt on his mother's face, her hunched posture worsened by the fight, her resolve weakened. Her pale light dimming ever so slightly. "Forgive me," he murmured.

"What the devil is going on here?" his grandfather said, coming into the room, the smell of pipe smoke following him. "Why are you raising your voice, Henry?"

"I was only . . ." he began. "I'm sorry. Please forget what I said, Mother." Silently he added, *You will, anyway.*

His mother stood up from the table, stacking the teacups and dessert dishes. "I accept your apology, however graceless."

"What was this all about?" Grandpa asked.

"A friend of Henry's stopped by to visit the farm a few days ago," Mother said, wiping her brow with the back of her hand. "I simply thought perhaps Henry would like to invite *the young lady* over for supper sometime."

"Well, that explains all the lunacy," said Grandpa. He shook his head and reached for the pile of dishes. "Girls."

Henry, frustrated, silent, went out the front door to the porch and plunked down into his mother's rocking chair. In the distance the mist was thick. And beyond it was Amy. He wondered if she'd come to see him again, after the way he'd explained everything. She probably thought he was some kind of ghost, some kind of liar.

Thinking about Amy, Henry wondered about the future, something he'd never allowed himself to do. It felt selfish. And it felt good. But merely for a moment, and then the familiar ache returned.

Henry rocked in the chair, missing his brother, and missing the person his mother used to be, back before everything had worn her down. He felt the burden of days heavier than ever. What would have happened to his family if he hadn't intervened that night? What would happen if time moved forward and he went away to war, only to face a fate similar to his brother's? Those fearsome thoughts had tempered everything since the endless summer began. But he'd held them off, storing them in the very back of his mind in favor of keeping everything the same as it was—as *safe* as it was.

The breeze started up, tickling the leaves on the trees and rustling through the laundry on the line. The now-familiar news report for this day drifted out from Mother's radio as his afternoon began unfolding in perfect synchronicity. Sighing, Henry forced himself back inside the house. Back inside the only life he knew.

CHAPTER ELEVEN

It's a party for the football team. Matt and I push through all the streamers and make our way to the kitchen. We're drinking from red plastic cups. Loud, loud music shakes the house. But then, things go crazy. Cop sirens wail. Kids run and suddenly, the basement seems to be the only safe place.

Matt and I smush into a closet with a bunch of other people. The hiding place reeks of beer breath and sweat and cologne. It's packed in there and Matt faces me. While we wait in the dark for the sirens to end and the noise upstairs to stop, Matt puts his hands on my stomach. In the sliver of light coming from the crack of the door, I can see Matt glance down at where he's touching me.

I start to say something, but Matt covers my mouth with one of his hands. "Shhh," he says, hushing me because of the cops, I guess. But then his other hand moves lower and I start to get nervous. I reach down and try to push it away, try to move back, but Matt holds me where I am. Matt's hand stays there, too. He's moving his fingers, trying to touch me through my jeans.

Someone behind us giggles like they know. I feel my cheeks get hot and scratchy. Matt keeps touching me. The cops are still upstairs, and I don't want to scream. I don't dare bite Matt's fingers over my mouth. I'm embarrassed. I start to breathe through my nose, sure I will pass out any second.

"Amy? Wake up, sweetie."

My eyes adjusted to the darkness of my room. The familiar smell of the trailer greeted me, the cracked-open window letting in damp air and blue-black night. I felt sticky, sweaty, and my heart was pounding.

Aunt Mae sat down next to me on the bed. She patted my clammy hand. "Nightmare. Katie woke me up whining to tell me about you."

I wiped my brow with the sleeve of my T-shirt and sat up against the pillows. "I was dreaming."

"You were crying out in your sleep," Mae said. She switched on the lamp next to my bed.

I took a deep breath. "Bad dream about before," I said. "About Matt."

"Bound to be some of those left in you. Let's go have a cup of tea."

"No, it's cool. I don't need anything," I said, hugging a pillow to my chest. I just wanted to go back to sleep, forget the dream, forget the parts of it that were true, the parts that made me feel used and dirty.

"My house, my rules," Mae said sternly.

Wiping my wet cheeks, I got up and followed her down the hall to the kitchen, knowing full well that tea wouldn't cure anything.

"I'll make us some chamomile," Mae said.

I sat down at the table, which was covered with books and boxes. Mae had been scrapbooking or something after I'd gone to bed.

"What's all this junk?"

Mae returned from putting on the kettle. "You got me thinking about the old place," she said. "I pulled out all my old photo albums." She got out her reading glasses and began flipping through dusty pages of a leather-bound book.

I saw a photo of the trailer—brand-new, with Mae next to it. She looked slightly younger, but she still wore her traditional overalls and her hair swept up into a loose bun.

"Look at me. Wasn't so long ago," Mae said, letting out a sigh. She flipped some more pages. "Oh, here's Dusty, my shepherd before Katie."

I took a look at the dog in the picture, a ringer for the one snoring on the floor near our feet.

Mae turned another page. "Okay, here's your haunted house. Very few pictures escaped the fire."

I peered at a much older photograph, black-and-white with scalloped edges. A run-down farmhouse. Henry's farmhouse. Paint peeling, sagging porch, a dark moss seeming to cover every slat of siding. It wasn't anything like what I had seen. The ghost house Henry inhabited was perfect, clean white, beautiful. But it was somehow the same house.

"That was the old Briggs place before we moved in," Mae said.

I felt goose bumps rise on my arms. "I know," I said. "I saw the house."

"You imagined it?" Mae cracked a smile. "Sweetie, I don't think places can be ghosts. Only people."

"Do you have any pictures of the family?"

Mae shook her head. "I don't have any pictures of them, sweetie." The teakettle whistled. "'Scuse me."

While Mae went off to get our tea, I flipped through more of the scrapbook, looking for more pictures of the house.

Mae came back to the table with two mugs of tea.

"I hate to tell you this—but I think your property is totally haunted by the Briggs family," I said, floating the truth.

"Wonderful," Mae said with a smile. "Years I complain about no one visiting me, and I had a whole passel of friends out back." She lifted her mug and blew on the hot tea.

"I knew you'd think I was nuts," I said.

She took a sip of chamomile. "No. I think you're creative. You taking up ghost hunting?"

"No, I guess not." I shut Mae's album and reached for my tea.

Mae set down her mug. "You know, you've been awfully quiet since your mom and Pete were here the other day."

"Meh, it's fine. Whatever," I said. I stirred some sugar into my tea. "I mean, it's not like they were around much, anyway."

"You say that, but I saw the look on your face that afternoon," Mae said. "I know you wish they weren't moving away, sweetie."

"Yeah, I thought I would go back home at some point."

Mae nodded. "It would be good for you to go back there, anyway. Someday, when you feel ready. If you avoid places or people, you give them power."

"Maybe."

Mae got up from the table, yawning. "I'm going to hit the hay. You going to be all right?"

"Yeah."

"Call Katie-dog up on the bed. She's an antidote to ghosts and nightmares. She wouldn't let anyone harm a hair on your head."

"'Kay. Thanks."

Mae shuffled off down the hall, and I opened the album on the table again. I finally found another picture of the house. This time the place was in ruins, scorched by fire. And there was the apple tree where I'd stood with Henry. I touched the picture, the edges curled and barely held down by the little black glued corners. I thought of him touching me. Holding me. And me feeling so safe.

"Why can't you be real?"

I shut the book and called Katie to bed. The ghosts in my life had haunted me enough for one night.

"Hey," Jackson said, sliding into the seat next to me in Mr. Planter's room for the homecoming meeting. "What's up with you? Tired or something? You've been yawning all day."

I shrugged. "Haven't been sleeping much."

"That I can tell. Bags under your eyes. Cute bags, but bags nonetheless," he said, winking.

I gave him a shut-it look and opened my notebook.

"Okay, let's get this meeting started. So, first of all, can we please do something cool for once?" Lori banged her fist on the table, silencing the other kids. They all stared at her.

Mr. Planter cleared his throat. "Cool is relative. What did you have in mind?"

"I know we usually do a theme at homecoming, but this year, since it's so close to Halloween, it should also be a costume ball."

"I like it," Mr. Planter said, nodding.

"That sounds fun," said Jackson.

Mr. Planter moved to the whiteboard. "Okay, any ideas for the theme?"

"Totally eighties!" Melanie, who'd come late to the meeting, piped up.

"That was last year's winter tolo theme," Lori said, rolling her eyes.

"Groovy disco seventies?" said the girl sitting next to me.

"The seventies is pretty overdone," Jackson pointed out. "And for the record, I'm not wearing polyester anything."

Mr. Planter chuckled. "I think you're on the right track. Let's keep thinking." He went to the whiteboard and started writing down all the suggestions in bright red pen.

Famous couples
Red, white, and blue
Greek mythology
Love through the ages
Literary characters

It was all clichéd. I didn't have anything new to contribute, but these weren't good. I tried to think back to school in Seattle—we'd done a seaside theme once, and another time something about a jungle. Lame and lamer.

"Movie scenes," called out Jackson.

"Uh, what? What's that supposed to mean?" Melanie said, giving him a withering look.

"You know—like we do some classic movies? Decorate the place like Hollywood, dress up. Have the paparazzi photograph us."

"You mean dress up like at a *Star Wars* convention?" offered Mr. Planter.

"Uh, no." Jackson held up two hands. "I was thinking like *Indiana Jones* or *Casablanca.*"

"Or *Breakfast at Tiffany's,*" I said, looking up from my doodling.

"Or *Legally Blonde,*" said Lori. "Yeah, that's cool."

Mr. Planter looked pleased. "Okay. So, do we have a consensus, team? The movies?"

Melanie groaned. "Oh, this is gonna suck."

Lori's smile faded.

"It's going to be fine," I said.

Melanie turned her annoyed glance to me. "I suppose you're going to do *Sex and the City*?" she said with a snarky laugh.

"Uh, what?"

"Never mind. Just something I heard," she said under her breath.

Mr. Planter capped his pen. "We'll meet again next week— how about next Tuesday, same time? Come prepared, and let's try to bring better attitudes," he said, giving Melanie a pointed look.

On the way out to the hall, I stopped Melanie. "What's your deal?"

"I'm not stupid," she said. "My friends told me they saw you drinking with Quinn on the back porch at Lori's party last Friday."

"Boy, your spies are everywhere," I said, shaking my head.

"I know what you're up to," she said.

"No, you don't. I'm not after Quinn. You don't have to worry about me."

"What? What do you mean by that?"

I saw something pained in her expression that almost made me feel sorry for her. How many other girls had she had to warn away from Quinn, since obviously he wasn't faithful? "Melanie, are you really happy with him, anyway? I mean, is he even nice to you?" I asked.

Her expression hardened. "Why are you even asking that? Look, I could make your life hell, so watch out and stay away from him. I know what girls like you are all about."

I bit my lip, wanting to say much more, but Jackson and Lori had caught up to us.

"Everything okay?" Jackson said, slipping an arm around my shoulder.

I didn't flinch. "Yeah."

Melanie raised her eyebrows and sashayed off down the hall.

"She's a one-woman rumor mill," Lori said. "I mean, not that she's starting anything about you. Just, you know . . ."

"No, I don't."

"Well," Lori said, sucking in a breath, "I heard Quinn's friends said some stuff about you and Quinn, but they make crap up all the time."

"What did they say?"

"They were talking about stuff you did at the party."

"Amy left the party early," Jackson said.

"I remember that, I think," said Lori, shouldering her bag. "Just watch your back. These rumors get started and have a life of their own."

"Well, maybe you could be a friend and help end them," Jackson said. He glared at Lori, and her cheeks flushed pink.

"No, it's fine. I don't even care," I said. "Really. It's not worth it."

Jackson shook his head. "I know you don't think much of this place," he said. "But I can't stand people making stuff up about my friends."

"You can always count on rumors in a small town," added Lori.

As we walked out in the parking lot toward Jackson's car, I saw Quinn getting into Melanie's hatchback. He gave me a sheepish smile as if to say, *I can't help it,* and then they drove off in a spray of gravel.

My stomach felt sick, but I held it together until I got to the safety of my room, where I buried myself under the covers. Why did people have to be so lame? Why did boys have to lie and start stuff? I hugged my pillow and missed home. And missed Mom. And truthfully . . . missed my ghost.

CHAPTER TWELVE

The chicken coop was warm that Saturday morning. Henry rolled up his sleeves and reached under the fat white hen, pulling out two bluish-tinted eggs. Things were starting to feel normal again. He'd thought about Amy less and less over the last few days as he fell back into the daily routines of the farm. He was trying to appreciate each moment they were given.

Next to him, Mother slipped another prize into her apron pocket. "That was a big one," she said, giving Henry a smile.

He nodded and moved down the line of nest boxes, placing more eggs into his basket, adding to the jumble of colors and sizes he'd collected.

"Isn't this marvelous? We have so many this morning," Mother said. Her pockets filled, she handed him one last egg. "Here, darling, you take this one. I'm all full up and I'd best go start breakfast. Grandpa will be up and grumbling any minute." She gave him a happy glance and for just a second, Henry glimpsed the Mother he'd known before the war, before his brother had shipped out. She hadn't always been as tired or sad as she was these days.

Henry moved toward the coop door, opening it for her.

"Such a gentleman," Mother said, with a bit of a bow. There was almost a giggle in her voice.

"What's got into you, Mother?" Henry asked.

"I don't know," she said, strolling out of the hen house. "I have a hopeful feeling today. Maybe we'll get one of Robert's letters in the post. We haven't had one in months. Since he was in England, I recall."

Henry knew that no letters would be coming. Not anymore. They'd stopped long before the day everything had changed.

"Yes, maybe a letter today," his mother said.

As Henry turned to latch the coop's door, he tried to remember if Mother had said those words before this summer began. Yes, but she hadn't been nearly as optimistic.

"Don't get your hopes up, Mother. It's hard for the men to write often," Henry said, catching up to her.

"Yes, that's true, dear." She reached up to touch a cluster of tiny apples on the tree. "Hmm . . . early for these yet," she said with a sigh.

And of course it was early for the apples, being that it was just toward the end of June. The immature apples, as much as the birthday cake the other day, were an early summer marker that came around each time. It was all part of the calendar that started over again, fresh and empty as a clean sheet of paper.

Henry followed his mother across the yard. He hadn't heard her humming in a while, and this morning it was a lofty Irish tune he remembered from his early years, something about springtime and green hills.

She mounted the porch steps jauntily, and in the yard behind them the rooster crowed. "And I bid good morning to you, sir," Mother said.

"Giddy. It's as if you're giddy," Henry muttered. And then he instantly thought of Mother's pills. Usually they didn't have this effect, but perhaps in the wrong dosage . . .

"All right, all right—I'll confess," Mother said in the kitchen, where she was emptying her pockets of eggs. "That lovely girl. Seeing you with her last week . . ."

Henry paused, his hands steadying himself against the table. Mother still remembered Amy. That hadn't happened before— she never seemed to hold memories from previous days of the summer. Then again, when nothing changed, no one stopped by the farm, nothing was different from any other day, what would that have given her to remember?

"The girl?" he repeated, prompting, since Mother had gone silent at the sink.

She turned around to beam at Henry. "Son, it gave me such hope! I could just picture a June wedding, a honeymoon at a mountain cabin. And I thought of Robert coming home and marrying a sweetheart of his own." She let out a sigh. "I dreamed of him last night, dear. I dreamed he was lying under the stars and thinking of us. Thinking of home. It gave me such a wonderful feeling, Henry. I woke up with joy in my heart."

Henry swallowed past the lump in his throat. "Mother, that's very nice, but there's a chance that he won't come back," he said. "The Eckingtons have already lost two sons in North Africa. Leon lost his cousin in the South Pacific. It's a dangerous war, especially with Robert so close to the Jerries."

"Don't say such things, dear. I felt him. He's safe. I feel it down in my bones. We just need to pray harder."

"I pray every night," Henry said.

"Yes. I hear you sometimes." She put some eggs into a bowl in the sink and then pumped water over top of them to wash the straw and dirt off the shells.

"You hear me pray?" Henry sat down at the table.

"Yes, though I don't understand the way you pray, son. Why do you ask for things to be the same, when Robert isn't here?" Mother turned to face him.

"You remember what I pray?"

"Of course, dear. I'm not senile." She laughed and began drying the eggs with a tea towel.

"But you don't remember other things."

"Such as?"

"What day of the week is it?" Henry asked.

"I'm pretty certain it's Saturday."

A glance at the calendar showed she was right; at least he thought she was. Lately it seemed he was measuring the days in terms of when he'd first seen Amy—and that had been two weeks ago Friday.

"I think I'd like to go to church tomorrow. Hopefully you'll come along with me," she continued.

"Mother, you haven't been to church in months and months."

"Well, I aim to go this week. I need to visit with the reverend's wife and take up a collection for your little friend. What was her name?"

Henry sighed. "Amy. There's no need to take up a collection, though. She won't be back." He didn't bother to mention Mother wouldn't be able to leave the farm to go to church, anyway. As far as he knew, Grandpa and Mother had never tried to leave—never needed to. Well, except for church, and Mother hadn't talked about church in forever. He didn't know what to make of that.

"Nonsense. She came all this way to the valley to see her relations, she can't be gone yet."

"Mother, please don't bother."

"Well, I think I may have something for her somewhere in my closet. At least something I can tailor for her," Mother said.

"No, ma'am. You don't understand. She won't return, I'm afraid."

His mother looked at him, aghast. "Why not? What on earth did you do to her?"

"Well, I guess you could say she doesn't like me anymore," Henry said.

"Well, that's unlikely. You're a charming, helpful young man. A girl would have to be plum crazy to dislike you," Mother said. She cracked eggs into the bowl and began to beat them with a fork. "Now, will you wake your grandfather, son?"

"Yes, ma'am. But, Mother, about church—you won't really go, will you?"

She paused at the window. "Oh, yes, I think I should," she said, turning back to Henry. "Poor dear looks like a ragamuffin out there on the path. Just standing there in the mist."

"How's that?" Henry joined his mother at the window.

"It's Amy," Mother said in a soft voice. "She's waiting for you."

He would have run to her if he weren't afraid that would scare her away again. Instead, he shut the back door behind him and walked up the path casually. But when he reached her, his voice betrayed him. "I've been hoping you would come back." He couldn't hide the emotion welling up inside him.

Amy took a tentative step forward from the clearing into Henry's sunshine-filled path. "Well, I wasn't going to, but I've been thinking about this place all week."

"I'm grateful you changed your mind," he said gently.

"Okay, so I'm coming over to your house whether you like it or not."

"Please, do," he said. "My mother saw you the other day. I'm pretty certain it's fine now. Nothing's changed, except you've got a standing invitation to dinner." He gave her a small smile.

"Is this place haunted?" Amy moved into the sunny morning, unzipping her jacket and tying it around her slim waist. It was an odd thing to do, not ladylike in the least, but Henry didn't care. He watched her face, her eyes, for signs that she'd run again.

"I said, is this a haunted house? Are you ghosts? Answer me."

He shook his head. "No ghosts here. It's my home. And it's always summer."

"And is your brother always away at war?" Amy said.

Henry shoved his hands in his pockets. "Yes." He looked up

at her and saw a flicker of something, pity maybe. "Right now—during this summer—he's over in France. As far as I know, as far as anyone here on the farm knows."

"And this farm?" Amy gestured at the house behind him, the green garden, and the lush, leafy apple tree. "What is this place?"

"I don't know. For a time, I thought it was heaven, but it's just our home. The same home. The same summer. And I'm here with my mother and my grandfather."

Amy took a step forward. "What year is it?"

"It's 1944. I tried to tell you the other day, but you ran off."

"Yeah, but it's not 1944. It's the freaking twenty-first century, Henry."

The twenty-first century. The words echoed in Henry's mind. He'd guessed Amy was from the future—but from the next century? He blinked at her, trying to comprehend what that meant. Of course, like all boys, he'd imagined what kind of world would exist in the future. Spacemen. Wondrous inventions. But he hadn't imagined the people. He couldn't have dreamed up anyone as congenial and pretty as Amy.

"You can't be real. This can't exist." Amy moved closer. "This is crazy. I feel like at any second you're going to disappear."

"I'm not going anywhere." Henry took Amy's hand.

She stared down in wonder. "You're touching me again. You're a ghost and you're touching me. How are you doing that?"

"I told you, I'm not a ghost."

Amy still looked fearful. "Can we go sit near the apple tree?" she asked, releasing his hand.

"Of course we can."

When they reached the tree, Amy reached up and touched one of the tiny apples sprouting from the withered cluster of blossoms.

"Those won't be ready. Ever." Henry took a seat on the bench near the tree, while Amy leaned against the trunk, watching him.

"I don't get this." She trailed her hand up and down the bark of the tree. She glanced back toward the path, toward the clearing, and Henry's heart seized. He couldn't let her run away again. He couldn't chance that he'd never see her again.

"I know it's hard to believe, but I'm as real as you. There was . . ." He stopped, wondering just how to explain what he hardly understood himself. "The end of June was difficult for my family. We lost my brother Robert at Normandy and then things got worse. I went to bed one night praying that life would go back the way it was before that night. I woke up the next morning and it was the beginning of summer again."

"From a prayer?"

"I never prayed before, really," said Henry. "Never asked for anything much. There was nothing I ever needed that badly."

Amy's brown eyes focused intently on his face. "So this pocket of time is some kind of miracle. I don't usually believe in miracles."

"I'm not a liar," Henry replied.

"I didn't say you were." Amy stepped away from the tree. She looked in all directions, turning in a circle to take in the farm and its surroundings. "Maybe this is all real," she said quietly. "If it's real, then it can't go away, right?"

"No, it won't go away," Henry said softly.

"Because that would really suck." Amy's eyes held that pain again, the pain that Henry wanted to touch, to cure.

"It would *suck*, huh? I guess that's your way of saying you wouldn't like it."

"Yeah." Amy's expression softened. "I'm so sorry about your brother, Henry. This whole thing is totally whacked. But the craziest thing of all is that I don't want this to be over. You're my only friend." She held her hand out toward him. "That's the only reason I came back."

As Amy's fingers wrapped around his, Henry felt a swell of

hope. He couldn't resist; he gently drew her into his arms. She softened against him, surrendering to the hug. He kissed the top of her head and said, "You're my only friend, too."

"And you won't disappear?" she whispered.

Henry sighed, lost in the scent of Amy's hair. "I'm not going anywhere."

CHAPTER THIRTEEN

Henry led me up the stairs of the back porch. The feel of his hand in mine was as real as the smells of biscuits and fried ham wafting through the air, as real as the sun on the back of my neck. I didn't know how, but he really was from another time. I didn't care how it was happening. I cared that he was standing next to me in that moment.

"Amy, please wait here," he said, and then he pushed open the back door and went in.

Through the window I could see a checkerboard-patterned kitchen floor and bulky white appliances. His mother, in a blue button-up dress and a flowery apron, paused from her work over the kitchen stove to speak with Henry. Then, she glanced up at me. She had the same sandy blond hair as Henry, the same blue eyes. I waved at her, and she waved back.

A second later, Henry came back out to the porch. "Amy, my mother would like you to have breakfast with us. Well, I would, too," he said, blushing slightly.

"Sure. I mean, I ate those amazing biscuits the other day. If they were old, they didn't taste like it."

Henry dipped his head closer to me and said, "As best as I can figure, in the clearing, time doesn't exist. Whatever we bring there just is. And now that you're on my side, it really *is* 1944. My mother, well, she doesn't quite understand what's happening here. So, when you speak to her, would you play along?"

I stared at Henry, not understanding. "She hasn't realized that this is the same summer?"

Henry shook his head. "She's a little confused lately, but she and Grandpa aren't aware of what's happening. I'm the one who set this in motion, so maybe that's the reason why."

"Oh," I said. "Um, do you think that's fair?"

"What do you mean?" Henry frowned.

"Well, just that you made this happen and it affected all three of you."

His frown softened. "You would have done the same thing. It was for the better. Someday, I'll tell you more."

"Someday? Sure." I shrugged. "Does someday even exist here?"

He guided me toward the door. "I think so," he said.

I stopped and looked Henry in the eyes. "Because if this is real—if this is all happening—then I want to know everything," I said. "It's important."

"Amy, I promise. Now, though, my mother is wondering what's keeping us."

"I'm really going to eat a 1944 breakfast with you?"

"Yesiree." He gave my hand a squeeze. "We're certainly not the Rockefellers though, so don't set your hopes too high."

My hopes were up, though. And that was a little scary. I was about to meet Henry's family: a family that was long gone from the earth, but not ghosts. A family I suddenly, desperately, wanted to like me.

"Come on. Mother's eager to meet you."

Henry escorted me through the door and into the kitchen. It was as real as anything. Bright sun coming in through the spotless windows. Ham sizzling in the pan. Henry's mother humming a sunny tune. The tink-tink of the old man at the table stirring his cup of coffee. The warmth of the oven shimmering all around us. A dizzying sense of everything hitting me at once. Henry's hand squeezing mine. This was real.

This was real. This was . . .

"There. Is that better, dear?" a woman's voice said.

I felt a coolness on my cheeks and forehead. I opened my eyes and saw friendly blue eyes.

Henry's mother dabbed my face again with the wet cloth in her hand. "Now, don't try to get up," she said. She set down the cloth and fixed the couch pillows behind my head. "Just rest. Henry is fixing you a plate."

I peered around the room. Dark wood bookcases lined one wall. A piano, its top covered with photographs, flanked a staircase. Across from me, a large picture window looked out toward the front yard.

"You fainted, Amy. Haven't your folks been feeding you properly?" Henry's mother gave me a kind smile and smoothed the bangs from my eyes. "Oh, here's my boy now with your breakfast."

Henry paused in the doorway, a plate in his hand and a concerned expression on his face.

I sat up. "I'm fine, really. I'll just eat with all of you at the table, ma'am." *Ma'am* sounded funny coming from my mouth, but I didn't know what else I would have called her.

As if it was a great struggle, Henry's mom slowly raised herself up from her seat on the edge of the couch where I lay, and then offered me a hand. She seemed frail, way too frail for me to accept it.

"That's okay," I said. I got up and followed her and Henry to the table.

"Well, you look a mite better," said the old man, with a little grin.

"Amy, this is my grandfather Briggs."

"Nice to meet you," I said, taking a seat opposite him at the table.

"Amy," Grandpa said. "Unusual name." He wore a light gray sweater over a blue shirt that looked homemade and round eyeglasses with metal frames. His face was kind, though his eyes held a weariness, just like Henry's mother's. "The pleasure's all mine," he added.

Meanwhile, Henry had slipped the breakfast he'd served up in front of me.

"Whoa," I said, eyeing the mountain of scrambled eggs, fluffy giant biscuit, and slice of ham piled on the china plate.

"Is there something wrong, dear?" asked Mother Briggs. She was shaking her napkin out and placing it on her lap.

I followed her example and did the same with the white linen cloth under my fork.

"I'm sorry," I said. "It looks delicious, seriously. Normally I just eat a bowl of cereal for breakfast. Or maybe some toast."

"Well, no wonder you're skinny as a rail," said Henry's grandpa with a wink.

Mother shot him a look. "Dear, what Grandpa means to say is that you must have a good meal first thing in the morning. Out here in the country, we're lucky to have enough to go around. Please, eat as much as you wish."

I eagerly took a bite of the biscuit. As flaky and buttery as the one Henry'd brought to the creek, this had to be the best baked anything I'd ever had. I set it back down on my plate and noticed everyone staring at me.

"Sorry, do I have crumbs on my face?"

"No," Henry said. "You had a giant smile," he said with a laugh.

Everyone started eating after that, or at least seemed to stop watching me eat, anyway. I piled a scoop of the scrambles onto the second half of my biscuit and took a generous bite. I washed it down with a sip of coffee. At least, I thought it was coffee. It was brown, anyway.

Henry noticed the sour look on my face. "We use the grounds several times," he said. "Coffee's rationed."

"Silly boy, of course she knows that," Mother said with a shake of her head.

"Right. Rations," I said, vaguely remembering that a lot of things were scarce back in wartime.

"Ah, but the first cup of the first brew is heaven," Grandpa said. "When it gets too weak, we resort to the burned carrots, or ground chicory when we can get it. Is that what you city folk are doing, too?"

I tried not to look too shocked. "Um, yeah, I guess. Burned carrots, though?"

"Tastes a bit like coffee," Henry said. "It's for the war effort. We've got to conserve whatever we can," he added with a nod to me.

"Oh, right. Yeah, I remember now."

"Amy, how could you forget?" Mother said. "I don't mean to rib you, but everyone's been on rations for the last few years. Surely your family has had to make do like the rest of us."

"Yeah, I mean, yes. I know, ma'am." I took another bite of biscuit, just so I wouldn't say anything else too stupid.

Grandpa Briggs saluted me with his cup. "How is your family? Henry's mother tells me you're staying with an auntie not too far away."

I glanced nervously at Henry, but he just nodded at me.

"Yes, sir," I said, wiping at crumbs with the linen napkin. "She's all the family I have here."

"What's her name, dear?"

"Mae."

"And her family name?" Grandpa said, his eyes alight with interest.

"Um, Johnson," I said.

"Johnson . . . Johnson . . . hmm . . ." He scratched the sides of his faintly stubble-covered cheeks. "I guess I knew a Vern Johnson who lived over on Jordan Creek once, but that's quite a ways away."

I didn't say anything. I knew from what Mae had said that her father didn't come to the valley until after the war, so it made more sense just to take another bite of eggs.

Mother got up from the table and returned with a glass jar. "Peach?"

"Um, sure," I said. "Please."

She scooped one glistening gold half onto my plate and then doled out one each to Grandpa and Henry. Capping the jar, she set it back on the counter.

"You're not having one?" I asked.

Mother wistfully smiled and took her seat. Her plate, which had been just half full, was still nearly half full. "No, dear. After canning that many last summer, I lost the taste for them, and of course, there'll be more to put up soon. Does your aunt can?"

"Can? Well, actually, yeah. I mean *yes*."

"That's wonderful. Canning is another way to help conserve," Mother said. "You know, Amy, speaking of conserving, new clothes are surely hard to come by during these times." Her voice dropped to almost a whisper as she leaned toward me. "But I may have some things for you upstairs, dear."

"Um . . ."

"It would give me great pleasure to send them home with you," Mother said.

I looked to Henry for guidance. "Um, well . . ."

Henry's cheeks had flushed bright red. "Mother, you don't have—"

"I insist, dear." His mom gave him a pointed look.

"Okay," I said. "It's fine, Henry."

"Good, it's settled, then," she said, dabbing her lips with her napkin. "Gentlemen, if you wouldn't mind excusing us, Amy and I will visit upstairs."

"Uh—"

"No, please don't protest, Amy dear. I won't hear of it." She got up from her chair and stood there expectantly.

I took a last bite of biscuit and then pushed out of the chair.

Mother slipped an arm around me. "Now then, let's see what we can do with you."

Hours later, I stood before the oak mirror in Henry's mother's room, barely recognizing my reflection. I was in a burgundy dress that nipped in at the waist and had short, gently puffed sleeves. Henry's mom had made a few alterations to the dress, and it fit perfectly. She'd also pinned my hair back on the sides into some reverse rolls and dabbed just a touch of her scarlet lipstick on my mouth. It'd been a long time since I'd played dress up, and even longer since my own mother had fixed my hair. I couldn't get over what a difference it all made. I felt a little weird, but I couldn't say I didn't feel pretty.

"You look lovely in that dark red," Henry's mom said, taking a seat on the bed. "I only wish I had some shoes to pass on to you."

"I know my feet are freakishly big." I looked down, wiggling the Converse Chuck Taylors on my feet. They definitely did not go with the outfit.

In this room with its dark wood furniture, floral curtains, quilted bed cover, and a pretty hand mirror and matching brush laid out on the dressing table, I felt like I was in a movie. But the clothes felt real enough on me, and my stomach was still full to bursting from our breakfast.

"That used to be my favorite dress. I sewed it from the Vogue pattern book a few years ago, before the war," Mrs. Briggs said.

I paused from admiring my reflection. "Are you sure you want me to have it?"

Her smile was slight but still there. "Yes, dear. It doesn't fit me anymore. It looks stunning on you."

I studied her, wondering how she must have looked. She was still beautiful, but thin. Maybe years of worrying about Henry's brother, or the food being rationed, had made her that way.

Seeming to notice my stare, she got up from her seat on the bed. "Now let me bundle these things for you. Are you sure your auntie doesn't need anything?"

"No. That's all right. I don't think she needs anything, thanks. In fact, I feel funny about taking these dresses."

"Oh, please don't fret about that," Mother said. "We all have to help one another. That's the only way we'll make it through these tough times." She looked down at the folded pile of jeans, sweatshirt, and tee on the bed—the things I'd worn over. "I'll bundle these work clothes for you, too." She gave me a gentle smile. "Really, Amy, you're a beautiful girl. You should play up your natural assets instead of wearing men's dungarees."

"Right."

She opened a drawer and pulled out a length of string to tie around my stuff to hold it all together.

"Mother?" There was a knock and Henry pushed open the door. "How are you—oh, holy cow."

"What? What's wrong?"

Henry paused in the doorway, steadying himself against the doorjamb. "You . . . you look—"

"Lovely. That is what my tongue-tied son is trying to say," his mother said, handing Henry my bundle of clothes.

He looked down at his shoes, his cheeks coloring. "Ah, yes. That's it exactly. Thank you kindly, Mother." He backed out of the doorway, letting his mom pass. I followed her, but Henry touched my arm as I moved toward the stairs. "I'm sorry. I didn't mean to stare," he whispered.

"It's okay."

"You look so . . . different," he said.

"I know. Is that a good thing?"

He nodded. "I'd pictured you, I mean, not that I'd pictured you, really—but I'd thought about what you might look like if you were from here. From now. And then, there you were. Like a dream."

I felt a hot flush hit my face. "Oh. Um . . . we should probably go downstairs," I mumbled.

"Yes," Henry said, but he didn't move.

I was suddenly aware of his hand on my arm, the soapy-clean smell of him so close again. "Should we go?"

Henry set the bundle of clothes on the banister. "Yes. Let's."

I turned to go, but his hand clasped mine. "What?" I said with a nervous laugh. "What's up with you?"

"What's *up?*" He pulled me closer to him and reached his free hand toward my chin. "When I'm around you, I can't . . . I want to . . ." He slid his fingers over my cheekbones, tucking a strand of hair behind my ears.

In the dim light of the upstairs hallway, I could see his eyes focus on my mouth. His hand still cupped my cheek. My heart raced as we started moving closer together. I closed my eyes. And then his lips touched mine.

So gentle. So, so gentle. He kissed me. Kissed me like he was afraid his lips would hurt mine. Kissed me so softly that my mouth tingled, anticipating, demanding more. And then he pulled away.

I opened my eyes and found him studying me. I cleared my throat. "Um . . ."

"Sorry," he said. "I didn't mean to."

"It's okay. I wanted you to."

"Amy . . ." he said, his voice trailing off.

I stood there, hoping he would kiss me again. Aching for him to kiss me again. To kiss me hard and fast and long. But he didn't.

"Come on." He picked up the bundle again and placed his free hand on the small of my back. "Let's get you home."

I went down the steps first, fully feeling Henry's eyes on me. I didn't know if he felt what I did. If he'd felt that wanting. A wanting that I hadn't felt . . . ever. All the times I'd kissed Matt Parker, I'd never felt that tingling anticipation. I'd never wanted him like I'd wanted Henry.

Silently, we walked along the path to the clearing. A few yards from the curtain of mist, Henry stopped. His gaze wandered over my face, pausing on my red lips. "I'm glad you visited today."

I fought back the blush rising in my cheeks. "Yeah, thanks for breakfast. And, um, thank your mom for me."

"She's watching us now," Henry said.

I looked beyond him and saw her in the kitchen window. I waved.

"Okay, well, goodbye, then," I said.

Henry handed me the bundle of clothes. "You don't have to take these dresses."

"No, it's all right," I said. "It was nice of her."

"Well, then." His eyes looked so blue then, against his tanned face and the background of the white house and the greens of summer. "You'll come again?"

"Yeah." I chewed my lower lip. *Kiss me. Kiss me. Kiss me.* My brain would not shut up about Henry. I wanted to kiss him. To sink into him. To cover myself with him. It scared me to want that.

"So long," he said, giving me a smile.

"Oh, okay. Bye, then," I said. I backed away down the path, not wanting to let go of the sight of Henry—until at last he turned and I watched him retreat toward the house. And then I pushed through the painful barrier into the mist, alone.

As I broke free at the other side of the clearing, I saw Mae standing at the edge of the woodlot. She leaned against a tree trunk, seeming to be catching her breath. "There you are," Mae said, her voice ragged. Katie, who was lying on the ground next to the tree, got up and ran over, sniffing me.

"What are you guys doing out here?" I asked.

Mae stared at me.

"What? Is something wrong? What's going on?" I asked. I searched Mae's concerned face for clues.

"Been calling you for lunch for half an hour," Mae said. "And would you like to tell me what happened to your clothes?"

I glanced down at my outfit. Right—I was in the burgundy dress. "Um, I was over at Lori's," I said, lying because it was so much easier than trying to explain the truth.

Mae gaped at me in disbelief.

"We're, um, doing a theme for homecoming," I said, thinking quickly. "It's the movies. I'm thinking of doing, um . . . *Pearl Harbor.*"

"Oh. I thought you were going to tell me you were ghost hunting in period costume," she said with a weak laugh.

"No. There aren't any ghosts," I said slowly. "I just cut through the field."

"The field? Well, suit yourself," Mae said, looking a little relieved. "You look very pretty in that dress. Come on now, we've got cheese sandwiches and tomato soup waiting—and that wood's not going to stack itself."

"Right, the wood," I said. "I keep forgetting the winter's coming." I wiped at the lipstick on my mouth with the back of my hand. Katie walked at my side, sniffing the dress like crazy.

Mae was moving slowly down the path. She paused at the wood pile, taking a seat on the edge of the chopping stump.

"You all right?" I asked, placing a hand on her shoulder.

Mae nodded, but her mouth was tight, and she was breathing heavily. "Just resting. I'll be fine. It's not easy getting old, sweetie."

"No, I guess not."

"When you're old, everything seems more difficult," Mae said. "Kind of like when you're a teenager."

"Yeah, right."

"I'm serious, Amy." Mae let out a sigh. "The physical things get more difficult when you're old like me, and the emotional things are hard when you're young like you. I remember when I was about your age; everything seemed like a crisis—everything was so big. Things happened that I thought I'd never get over."

"Yeah?"

Mae nodded. "Had my heart broken. Lost loves. Said goodbye to people I was sure would be in my life forever." The wrinkles around Mae's eyes deepened. "At my age, it's all distant. But at yours, hurt is fresh and deep as anything."

I tilted my head thoughtfully. "Mae, I always wanted to ask you—why did you choose to live out here alone? I mean, you did choose this, right?"

Mae glanced up at me, her blue eyes watery. "Yes and no," she said in a soft voice. "When I was just a baby we lived in a small house downriver—near the town of Sedro. Daddy always wanted a piece of real land, but this was during the Great Depression and we couldn't afford much. My sisters and I grew up downriver, watched so many of our friends get married right out of school, or go off to college to find a husband if their families could afford the tuition. I had my eye on a young man back then. Then the war came, and most of the boys in town, and some of the fathers, went off to fight. And the boy I loved—his name was Joseph Hansen. My Joe was drafted into the Marines."

"And," I said, my throat feeling tight, "what happened?"

"He didn't come back."

"Oh."

"I never married, didn't plan on it, anyway. Joe had been the only one I'd ever loved. I didn't think I would find anyone else who would make me feel the way he did. And I was right."

"Mae, that's so sad."

She laughed and wiped at her wet eyes with her sleeve. "It's ancient history now, Amy. That's what I mean about being old—it gives you distance. When you're going through something, especially at your age, it seems as though you'll never survive. But you will."

I didn't know what to say that would make Mae feel better. For all her talk about the years giving you distance from the pain, it sure didn't seem to be true for her. She'd lost a love back when she was my age, and it still haunted her.

Without the summer sun on my skin, I shivered in the short-sleeved dress. I set the bundle of clothes on the woodpile and dug out my sweatshirt. I pulled it on over the dress, not caring how odd it must have looked. Without the happy glow I'd felt over at Henry's, I was cold.

"You have fun at Lori's?" Mae asked, trying to sound cheerful, though her eyes still held pain.

I nodded, feeling guilty for my lie. "Yeah, sorry, I guess I should have told you I was going out."

"I'm not angry, Amy. It's good that you have made some friends."

"Yeah," I murmured. Impossible friends.

"You look far away, sweetie," Mae said.

I felt far away. Henry kissing me was still fresh in my mind, but so was Mae's sad story. "I guess I feel worn-out, just like you," I said.

"Well, it's good to hear you're having fun with your friends instead of poking around after nonexistent ghosts."

"Yeah, I won't be poking around after them anymore," I said. I totally meant it, since there weren't any ghosts. There were only

Henry and his family, and they were as real and as caring as anyone I'd ever met.

"There you go again," Mae said, rising from the stump. "Faraway girl. You sure there wasn't a boy over at Lori's? You have that look in your eyes."

I laughed, in spite of myself. "I don't know what you're talking about."

"You can't kid a romantic like me." She moved toward the back steps. "But for now, soup is calling us."

I climbed the stairs behind her, watching her choose each step carefully and grasp the railing like a liferope. Most of the time, it was easy to forget that Mae was old since she had such a vibrant personality. Observing her in this moment, though, there was no hiding her age.

I took my precious cargo of dresses into my room, unpinned my hair, changed back into my jeans, and then hung up the three dresses in the closet one by one. Burgundy, blue with white trim, floral pink. I stared into the simple mirror on the back of my door. In the wan, gray light flooding my room, I was just another girl with boring brown hair, a skinny build, and plain clothes.

I reached into the closet and took out the deep red dress again, holding it up against me. I longed for the Amy Henry saw, had made me see. I wanted to be colorful, to be alive. I wanted to be with the boy I was starting to ache for. The boy who made a single kiss feel like my first. I wanted to be in an endless summer with Henry Briggs.

"Hey! Wait up!" Jackson hailed me outside of the town library after school on Monday. "Didn't you get my texts? I was gonna see if you wanted a ride over here."

"Oh, sorry." I paused to let him catch up and fumbled in my bag for my cell. "Oh, yeah," I said. "I never turned my phone on after this morning. I keep forgetting."

"There is technology up here in the so-called sticks, Amy," Jackson said, giving me a look of doubt.

"Yeah," I said, shoving my phone back in my bag. "So, Lori's coming, too, right? I mean, if we're doing this movie theme, then we really should check out all the options."

"Yeah, this is way better than the school library . . ."

"Okay, what? You're staring. Do I have something on my face?"

Jackson was looking at me, not in a disapproving way, but still. "You doing something different with your hair?" he asked.

I reached up and touched the barrette that was holding a section of my hair back in a wide wave. "Um, I just got sick of my bangs being in my face all the time."

"It looks pretty," he said in a thoughtful tone. "Kinda retro, and I can see your eyes better."

I smiled.

"And now you look even prettier. Wait—you might even look happy if I squint my eyes a little," he said with a laugh. Jackson slid his backpack off his shoulder and leaned against the wall of the entryway. "So this place isn't sucking as bad as you thought at first?"

"It's not without its charm," I said. Out in the parking lot, the rain started pounding into the already-full puddles. October was here in a big, wet way.

Jackson popped a stick of cinnamon gum into his mouth and held one out to me. "So, you think this dance is actually gonna be fun."

"Yeah, I guess." I unwrapped the gum.

"I'm not going with Shelli, you know, my ex." Jackson balled the foil paper in his hands.

"Yeah, the one from the party, right?"

Just then, Quinn and Melanie came out of the drive-in across the street, carrying to-go bags. Quinn saw us outside of the library and gave me a wave before ducking into the passenger side of Melanie's car.

"Ugh," I muttered.

"Hmm, so it's not Quinn," Jackson said.

"It's not Quinn, what?"

"Well, I just thought maybe you're, um, hanging with someone. You seem distracted and maybe even kinda happy-ish."

"I'm just plain old me. Quinn-free as always," I said, shaking my head.

"Well, cool, 'cause I was thinking that maybe . . ." His blue eyes sparkled a little and his mouth quirked at the corners. "Amy, I suck at this. I'm just trying to ask you to the dance."

"Oh," I said.

"She hesitates," he said. "Not good."

I swallowed back the sudden lump in my throat while Jackson stood there anticipating my answer. I liked him, so why shouldn't I just go? I mean, it wasn't like Henry was coming over to my side to be my date. Seriously.

"We can go, you know, as friends, if you want to," Jackson said. He stuffed his hands in his jeans pockets.

"Um, who else is going? I mean, are we going as a group of friends?"

His smile flattened. "Um, yeah, we could do that. I mean, I don't think Lori's got a date, and probably her friend Mindy would want to go with us . . ."

"Okay. Yeah, that'd be good," I said.

"Cool." Jackson picked up his backpack. "I'll be happy to be there, even as your friend."

My heart cracked a little. "Jackson, you're sweet. Stop it, 'kay?"

He chewed his lower lip, looking at me like he was trying to figure out what I meant. At last he said, "Oh, hey, I meant to ask if you have a problem with James Bond. You know, I know he's kind of a womanizer, but he's also—"

"What?"

"Agent 007. I was thinking you could be a Bond girl, and well, Lori and Mindy, too."

"I really wanted to do *Pearl Harbor*," I said, touching the wave of my hair. "You know, retro?"

His smile reappeared. "Yeah! And I could be a GI and you all would be some USO girls or something."

"Or something," I said, giving him a pat on the shoulder.

"That's good," he said. "I like it. With your hair like that, I can just picture it. You'll look great, Amy."

My cheeks got all scratchy. "Um, yeah," I said. "Just don't tell everyone about our plan, 'kay? And we have to tell Lori to keep quiet, because I don't want anyone to copy us."

"Oh, don't worry—I heard Quinn and Melanie are doing monster movies—*Frankenstein* and *Bride of Frankenstein*."

"Nice."

"Yeah, but I can't imagine Melanie going all monster ugly."

"Hmm, I don't think it would be too hard." I started into the library.

"Hey," Jackson said, catching me by the hand. "Whoever he is, he's lucky, Amy. Very lucky."

"I don't know what you're talking about," I said.

He winked. "You can't lie about stuff like that. I see you."

I shrugged off his comment. "Can you give me a ride home after this?"

"I'd be honored," he said, and then let me go.

"If we're doing this, it has to be perfect," Lori said, flipping through another volume on World War II. She had a huge stack of books next to her on the table. The old guy at the circulation desk had been more than happy to help us research. "Look at this dress! I wonder if my mother can sew it for me in time for the dance."

Jackson groaned. "Lori, I'm all researched out. Can't we just watch *Pearl Harbor* and take notes?"

"Yeah, maybe that's a good idea. My eyes are glazing over here," I said. "They have great costumes in the movie."

"Um, hello—that's a modern interpretation of the forties," Lori said. "This is a really awesome idea, Amy, and I want everything to be perfect. Can you imagine everyone's faces when we walk in and look like a million bucks? Come on, let's shoot for ten more minutes."

"You said that ten minutes ago," Jackson said.

Lori glared at him. "Don't forget, we're in charge this year. If we don't rock it out, then that's not going to happen again."

"When did you turn into such a tyrant?" Jackson said, laughing. "It's like you're drunk with power."

Lori smiled, like she thought it was a compliment. "Back to work."

Jackson held up his hands in surrender. "Sure thing, boss."

I had to hand it to the girl; she was motivated. "Ten minutes," I said, shaking my head. "Slide over," I said to Jackson, who was manning the computer station near our worktable.

"There's nothing here," he said. "The *Skagit River Reporter*'s archives on the forties suck."

I checked out the webpage Jackson had found, noting the paper had gone under a couple of years ago, which was probably why the site wasn't the greatest.

"And honestly, it's depressing looking at all the articles about the guys who were my age and died," Jackson said.

"There were a lot of those." I turned back to the computer and clicked on the Veterans section. I scanned down the huge list of names from World War II. And then I came to one that made me pause: *Robert Briggs.*

I clicked on it and a photograph popped up. I expected it to be of a young army soldier killed at Normandy in 1944, but instead it was a picture of an old man.

An old man who had died *only five years ago.*

I hit Print.

CHAPTER FOURTEEN

Henry plucked another blade of grass and stuck it between his teeth, chewing the milky sweetness from the stem and remembering that magical afternoon at the creek with Amy, an afternoon that seemed a lifetime ago. Leaning back in the grass, he looked up at the summer sky, trying to see the dragons and castles they'd found together. Nothing but big, puffy white clouds today. Giving up, he closed his eyes, letting the sun warm his face. What he wouldn't give to have Amy next to him in the grass, to touch her silky hair that smelled of strawberries and wood smoke.

He heard a rustling sound—movement along the path from the clearing. His heart beat a little quicker as he anticipated Amy's presence.

"Henry? You out here?" His grandfather's voice sailed out through the bushes, and a second later, the old man emerged with a tackle box and a couple of fishing rods.

"Yes, sir. Over here," Henry said. He couldn't keep disappointment from his voice.

"Fishing's a fine way to spend a Saturday afternoon, but it's a mite hard to catch anything when you leave your fishing gear behind." His grandfather set down the box and leaned the poles against the willow's trunk. "I brought a pole for you and one for myself."

"You followed me?"

His grandfather nodded. "Yes, well, I saw you headed this way."

"But you never come down to the creek," Henry said, slowly.

His grandfather raised the brim of his straw hat. "Yes, that's so—but you've been spending a lion's share of your time out here or in the foggy swamp. I figured there must be something special to it. This your secret fishing hole?"

"Not really."

Grandfather took a seat next to Henry. "Maybe we could toss out a couple lines."

"That'd be fine." Henry got up and dug around in the tackle box so he could rig up the rods.

"You know, Henry, it's a bit odd out here," Grandpa said, watching him work. "It's queer coming through the mist, cold and lonesome. I can't say I prefer it to the farm."

"Hmm," Henry murmured, not wanting to start on that discussion.

"This fog hasn't always been here."

Henry paused, tying the leader on to the fishing line. "What do you mean?"

Grandfather gave him a hard look. "I hadn't thought about it until recently, but that fog rolled in across the field—well, really around the whole farm—sometime after spring began. I'm certain of it."

"And what made you think of that?" Henry said, going back to working on the rod. He ignored the dry feeling in his mouth.

"That little gal, Amy, was the first visitor we've had on the farm in ages. I hadn't thought to walk down the road to check on any of the neighbors in quite a long time, but visiting with Amy got me thinking about the Widow Barnes and her sick calf. I remembered promising her I'd pay her a visit. I started down the road toward her piece yesterday while you were out in the garden. When I came to our fence post, the one that divides our parcel from the county road, there was nothing but this gosh darn fog there, as far as I could see."

"We don't need to leave the farm, Grandpa." Henry turned his attention to rigging the second pole. "Her calf's probably fine now."

"But why the fog, Henry? I didn't walk through it, but it gave me pause. When did that fog roll in around the whole farm?" Grandpa gestured to the creek, where the fog was like a huge white veil over the opposite bank.

The confusion in his grandfather's face scared him. Henry finished rigging the fishing lines. "Here you go," he said, holding out one of the rods.

Grandpa took it, but made no move to get up to fish. "I have vague recollections of you trying to explain things, the fog and the like, to me. I didn't fall off the last turnip truck. You know what's going on, son."

Henry felt a strange feeling in his stomach. "I did try to tell you, sir. I did try to tell you when all this began." He didn't say that things were changing now, that probably Amy had started all this. It didn't feel right to blame her for it. Amy had only brought him happiness, but maybe that happiness had a price. Henry pushed the thoughts of her aside, as difficult as that was, and forced himself to focus on his grandfather.

He started with the truth. "I wanted things to stay the same. I wanted Mother to be well. I wanted the three of us, all the Briggs family there is, to stay together. That's how all this happened."

"*Three* of us. There are four of us. Your brother may be out of sight, but he's not out of mind."

Henry's chest tightened. *Yes,* he wanted to say, *Robert is no longer in this family.* But instead, he said, "You're right. He's never out of my mind, sir."

"Well, I don't see how your explanation makes a lick of sense." Shaking his head, Grandpa stood up with the fishing rod and walked to the edge of the stream. "You wanted all of these things for us? These were your boyhood desires that brought the mist. How does a change in weather concern your mother's health or our family's staying together?"

"Boyhood desires? It has nothing to do with boyhood desires," Henry said. "I prayed for something that would help our family."

"Prayed?" Henry's grandpa cast out his line. "The Lord doesn't answer prayers with fog."

"Well, perhaps this time he did, sir." Henry took up his rod and joined his grandfather at the stream. "Perhaps there are a whole host of things happening to us because of my prayer." He cast the lure out, jigging it in slowly to entice the Dolly Varden from under the rocks.

Grandpa sighed deep and long. "Look, son, all I know is, I haven't seen another living soul in ages. Seen you and your mother and this little gal, Amy, and that's it. What happened to the town? What happened to us?"

It's what didn't happen, Henry wanted to say. But instead, he kept fishing, and let his grandfather's question float on downstream.

The after-supper pipe smoke was a distant phantom floating out from the back porch to the bean patch. Henry watched the white specter join the mist coming from the clearing. And then, as he and Grandpa listened to the chorus of grasshoppers start up over the string orchestra on the radio, they got out the checkerboard.

The conversation at the stream seemed to be put to rest for the time being. Grandpa hadn't asked any more questions, and Henry had been relieved. He dreaded telling Grandpa what was to happen to Robert. He was half afraid that Grandpa wouldn't believe him—and half afraid he would. Then Mother would find out, and everything would come apart. Everything Henry had sought to save his family from would come to pass.

The Dolly Varden he and Grandpa had caught had been enough to get Grandpa's mind off bigger topics. Back at the house, Mother had dusted the fish in cornmeal and fried them to a golden brown. She'd seemed happy to have something fresh for supper, and had even put together a parfait from the new strawberries coming on in the garden.

"Well now, look here—she walks in beauty," said Grandpa, gesturing with his pipe. Henry looked up from setting out the checkers and saw Amy strolling out of the mist and onto the path to the house.

She was dressed in one of his mother's hand-me-down dresses—the blue shirtwaist—but on Amy, it looked like new and fitted perfectly. Instead of leaving her hair loose, she'd fashioned a pretty ponytail and combed her bangs to one side. She moved into the porch light, and Henry noticed the lack of sparkly eye makeup on her face. She looked natural, bare, except for a rosy red shade of lipstick. If he hadn't known better, he'd have easily thought she was a schoolmate, or a girl from the town.

He was struck by how easily she could blend into his world, but at the same time, he was painfully aware she could never truly be of their time.

"Well, good evening, Miss Amy." Grandpa rose from his chair as she approached.

Henry followed suit, abandoning the checkers. "Hello, Amy."

"Oh, don't get up—I didn't mean to interrupt anything," Amy said softly.

"Nonsense. A lady approaches; gentlemen rise." Grandpa gave Amy a wink and then settled back into his rocker seat. "What brings you down our piece of road this fine evening?"

"Just visiting, I guess." She gave Henry a shy, uncertain look.

Suddenly, Henry thought of the kiss on the stairs and wondered if Amy was angry with him for taking such liberties. "Nice of you to visit again," he said, feeling unsure of himself.

Amy's smile faltered, for an instant. "Yeah, well, I wanted to come over. I needed to, um, talk to you."

The nervousness in Henry's stomach intensified. She was angry, he supposed. And rightfully so. What was he doing kissing her, when it was impossible—*they* were impossible?

"Please excuse me, Amy. I was just about to go trouble Henry's mother for a bit more dessert," Grandpa said, rising from his chair. "Would you like me to fetch you some?"

"Oh. Sure . . . um . . . yes, please. Her cooking is so yummy."

Grandpa grinned at Amy. "If that's what you young people are calling *delicious* these days, I'd have to agree." He went into the house, the screen door banging closed behind him.

Amy took a seat next to Henry on the porch swing. She smoothed the dress over her legs.

He moved closer to her, close enough to touch, but she kept her hands in her lap. "You look so pretty tonight, Amy. Mother's in the kitchen. I know she'd be tickled that you're wearing the dress she gave you."

"Thanks," Amy murmured, her gaze lowered.

Henry worried again that she really was upset about the kiss. "Say, what's the big idea about coming over at night?" He played off his fear with a little laugh. It sounded weak, even to his own ears.

Amy shrugged. "I had to see you. I had to wait until Mac went to sleep. I don't want her worrying about me."

"It's awfully dark out there. Weren't you afraid to cross the clearing?"

"Scared of what? Disappearing into the mist? I've never been scared of that."

He nodded. No, Amy didn't seem scared about the clearing. Then again, she hadn't anything to lose.

She fixed him with a stare. "Look, there's something we need to talk about," she said.

"I figured you were sore at me," Henry said. "It's just that when I was with you in the hallway, I couldn't control myself. I hope you'll accept my apologies."

"It's not that," she said. "That was all right."

"Good." Henry exhaled and reached for Amy's hand. "I'd never do anything to hurt you, Amy. I'd never jeopardize . . . well . . . this."

"Right. This." Amy's smile faded away. "I'm not sure what *this* is."

"Yes. Good point. It's a little confusing, isn't it."

"Yeah."

"Then why does it feel so right when you're with me?" Henry stroked Amy's hand in his, and she moved closer to him on the swing, resting her head against his shoulder.

"I don't know, Henry," she whispered, "but this can't last."

Henry wanted to pretend he hadn't heard what she'd said, but his throat went dry. He didn't want Amy to think that way. He didn't want anyone to think that way. "We have this moment. We have this time together now."

"Sorry to be a downer, but what if this time now isn't enough?"

"It's all I have. It's all I can give you."

Amy searched his face and Henry steeled himself for what was to come. His deepest fear was that Amy would tell him she was never coming back, and yet somehow, he couldn't believe she would do that. Sitting next to her on the swing's bench, the slow movement rocking them together, the sounds of the orchestra on the radio sailing out like a serenade, the moment was perfect. He couldn't believe she would risk destroying that with pragmatism.

"What's on your mind, then?" Henry asked. "I know I've been thinking about you."

Amy let out a sigh and looked up at Henry with a crooked smile.

"What? Did I say something funny?"

"No, it's just that I can't believe it when you say things like that to me."

"What do you mean? Do you think I'd lie?"

"No." Amy chewed her lower lip. "But guys don't usually mean it when they say stuff like that."

"Am I just some *guy?*" Henry said, sounding hurt.

"I don't mean it like that," Amy said. She sat up straight on the swing bench, making Henry feel farther away. "You're not just some guy." She folded her arms across her chest. "But some of them have said some pretty lame things."

Henry couldn't hold back this time. "This boy," he said, "the one who really broke your heart—I'd like to break his legs."

"Maybe it was my own fault. Maybe I made some dumb choices," she murmured.

"Loving someone isn't dumb," Henry said. "I mean, I don't know a whole lot about love, but I don't think it's dumb if it's real."

"But how do you know what's real?" Amy said. She unfolded her arms and leaned back into the swing. "I mean, at the time, I thought things were real between me and this guy—Matt. I thought he really cared about me. He made me feel special, I guess. But then I found out that everything had been a lie, that he wasn't who I thought he was."

"We're always who we are," Henry said. "Mostly people don't show you all sides of themselves. I'm pretty sure it's impossible to become someone else suddenly. Human nature is to hide the parts that aren't pretty to look at. It's easier to hide than to be your ugly real self," Henry said.

"Yeah, well, some people hide a whole lot of ugly," Amy said with a bitter laugh. "I moved to my aunt's to get away from Matt and everyone. To start over somewhere where nobody knew me." Her eyes looked fiery in the porch light. "I didn't think I would find someone like you. I mean, this wasn't what I was expecting.

I don't think most people would believe this was real like I do, anyway. I have a hard time believing it myself."

"But this *is* real. It couldn't be more real. I don't think anyone could make up the way I feel about you, or could dream it up, even," Henry blurted out.

Amy's cheeks darkened with a blush.

"Oh, gosh. Sorry, I don't mean to keep saying the wrong things," Henry said, shaking his head. "I'm a heel. All I have to do is open my mouth and these stupid words fall right out."

"But they're not stupid. That's the problem," Amy said softly.

Henry took her hand in his. "I can't help it. I've never met a girl like you before. Never, well, never felt like this, I guess."

Amy closed her eyes, leaning into Henry. "Me neither," she whispered.

Henry lifted her chin, noticing tears on her cheeks. "Don't cry, Amy. I don't mean to make you feel bad," he said. "Did I say something stupid again?"

"No. It's just . . . look, I have to tell you something. I have to tell you something, and I'm afraid all of this will end—that you will go away when I tell you. I'm afraid of what will happen to us. God, did I just say *us?* I must be crazy." Amy swiped at her tears with the back of her hand, but Henry stopped her.

"I'm not going to leave you," Henry said, kissing her tears. "Now that I found you, I don't see how I can let you go."

The screen door banged open and shut. "Here we are, Miss Amy. Strawberries for the prettiest little girl around," Grandpa said, coming out with a tray of dessert. He caught sight of Amy's expression and turned to glare at Henry. "Brought one for your *cad* of an escort, too."

Henry straightened up on the bench, and Amy sniffled away the last of her tears.

"Oh, my dear Amy, I should have warned you," Grandpa said,

handing her a glass parfait dish and a spoon. "I've done my darned-est to raise a gentleman, but it looks like my lessons didn't take."

Henry rolled his eyes and reached for a dish of dessert. He really wanted to keep speaking with Amy, but strawberries would have to do for now. He couldn't imagine what was on her mind, but he feared she'd finally decided that she wouldn't come back, couldn't. If that was the case, he was glad of the interruption.

"No, he's being a gentleman," Amy said.

"Hmm. Well then, if you're not the cause of Amy's long face, I apologize, Henry. And Amy dear, have some strawberries; they ought to cheer you up." Grandpa saluted them both with his spoon, and then the three of them dug into the parfaits.

"I meant to compliment you on how lovely you look tonight, Amy," Grandpa said. "I asked Alma, that's Henry's mother, to come out and say hello. She's resting in the parlor now, but she said she'd like to visit with you. She's lonely for a woman's com-pany," he added.

"She doesn't have many friends out here?" Amy asked.

Grandpa nodded. "Used to have quite a few, but recently, well, all summer, the folks just seem to stay away. Caught up with the war effort and their own families, I reckon." He took another bite of strawberries and gave Henry a pointed look.

Henry raised his eyebrows at his grandfather. "How is your parfait, Amy?"

She clinked her spoon back into the nearly empty dish. "Very good."

"Mine, too," Grandpa said. "I'll go see if Alma can come on out."

"Oh, that's okay," Amy said. "Just tell her hello from me."

Grandpa collected the dishes. "Henry, you behave out here," he said, carrying the tray off to the kitchen.

Amy turned to Henry. "Walk me to the clearing," she said.

"So your grandpa and mom don't know what's going on, right?" Amy said. "So why did your grandpa say that thing about no one coming around?"

Henry slowed on the path, stopping at the apple tree. "He's changing, Amy. He and my mother, both. All these summers, all these days, we've lived them the same and they've never questioned it. In fact, they didn't believe me when I told them what was happening."

"Isn't that a good thing, then, that they're finally getting what's going on?"

"I don't think so," Henry said slowly, watching Amy's face in the faint light.

"Why not? I don't get it."

"I always felt that this was fragile," Henry said. "At any moment the bubble could burst and everything bad would unfold—all of it."

"But you don't know that everything bad unfolds."

"Oh, yes—I know," Henry said. "I don't want to live through that night with my mother again. She couldn't take the bad news about my brother."

Amy studied him, and Henry was glad she didn't ask questions about what had happened. He didn't know if he could bear to think about it, let alone repeat it all out loud. He closed his eyes and smelled the sweetness of the apple tree on the breeze, the warm scent of earth coming up from the garden. Music from the house drifted out over the backyard—Glenn Miller playing "Stardust"—the strains of the orchestra floating all around him in the dark.

"So you're holding all this together with a prayer."

"I was, I mean, I am," Henry said. "It's been different for me lately. Different since you came along." He opened his eyes and found Amy looking at him with a serious expression, her mouth a thin line.

Amy glanced back toward the house. "Don't you ever wonder what would happen if you went forward? Don't you think people have the ability to change—to choose different outcomes?"

"If I went forward . . ." Henry repeated. The breeze rustled the leaves on the tree, and goose bumps pricked on his forearms. "If we went forward, nothing good would come of it."

"What if you went through the clearing to my time?" Amy asked, her voice softening. "I mean, what if you came into my world? All of this is wonderful, but if I can come through to see you, can you come through to my side?"

Henry gave her a small smile. "I don't think crossing the clearing would be a good idea, though. I don't know for certain it would work for me. What if I couldn't get back? What if something happened to Mother or Grandpa over here, and I was stuck? I can't risk that."

"Are you going to tell me what's so awful about reaching the end of the summer? What is so terrible that you would stop everything from happening?" She looked about to say something else, but held it back.

Henry's jaw clenched. "My mother, Amy—she's not well." He wanted to tell her more, but he worried that if Amy did come back, she might say something in front of Mother, something about Robert, and that would push Mother over the edge again.

"And to keep her well, you'd deny yourself the opportunity to move forward with your life. I mean, don't you want to go off to college, have a great career, get married, have a family someday?"

Henry's heart clenched in his chest. He did wish for those things—had found himself wishing for them more than ever since he'd known Amy. But there were other things keeping him from realizing those wishes, other things holding him back. "Amy, I'll most likely be drafted this summer."

"So," she said softly, "you'll be shipped overseas to who knows where."

Henry nodded. "Our boys took Normandy. I imagine it will be Europe."

"Or the Pacific," Amy said.

Henry shrugged.

"So you'd stay this way—here—eighteen your whole life, not experience anything, not see the world."

"I have the people I love with me."

"But you don't get a chance to love anyone else," Amy said.

Henry said, "Well, maybe yes, maybe no."

Amy didn't say anything for a moment, and Henry wished he could take back his bold comment. He didn't know what right he thought he had to presume this was love, or if Amy would even love him back. And obviously, he'd made her uncomfortable. She wouldn't look at him.

"What if all this disappears with a change of your prayer? Then what good was it?" Amy said, finally breaking the torturous silence.

"Loving someone is never a waste, Amy." He reached for her hand.

"What if the truth makes this all go away?"

"What kind of truth could do that?" Henry pulled Amy into his arms and finally said what he'd been holding back. "What did you come here to talk to me about, anyway? Are you going to tell me you're not coming back?"

"I don't want to tell you anything. I don't want any of this to end."

"Are you going to tell me something happened with Matt? Because I don't care about that. I don't care about whatever happened before; I just want to be with you."

"But if you can't cross over and be with me in my lifetime,

then we can't be together, can we? I mean, you plan to go on living this way forever, and I have to move on. I have to go to school tomorrow, and grow up, and move away to somewhere eventually. I can't come to the field forever, can I?"

Henry kissed her. Kissed her to shut her up because he couldn't take any more of the what ifs. Couldn't take any more thoughts of Amy's not being there with him.

"No," Amy said, pulling away, her eyes fierce. "You can't just kiss me and think all of these questions and problems disappear."

"Why not?" he asked, reaching up to stroke her cheek. "You make me forget everything, and it's lovely," he said. "Being with you is the first different thing in my life. Before you, I didn't think about anything other than this summer. I didn't want anything else . . ."

"Henry. Seriously."

"You wrecked all this for me."

"Yeah, that's what I do best, wreck things," Amy said.

"I didn't mean it that way," he said. "I think you know that."

"Do I? And what if I knew something that would *really* wreck things—all of this? Do I just keep it to myself? 'Cause when I cross that clearing, when I go back to the super fabulous trailer on the other side, all I think about is *you*. That's the awful truth, Henry. That's more awful than anything."

Amy walked off toward the clearing, leaving Henry standing there stunned. He didn't—nearly couldn't—move. The prospect that Amy could be having the same feelings as he was weakened him.

"Amy!" Henry called after her. In seconds he was beside her in the mist, pulling her into his arms. "Don't say something like that and run off," he said, kissing her forehead. "Don't."

"It's going to be too hard." Amy looked up at him, and Henry saw she'd been crying again.

"No, no—none of that," Henry said, stroking the tears away with his fingers.

Her eyes were half closed and she was shaking her head slowly. "This is all going to go away and it's going to be really hard for me to deal."

"Then don't make it go away," Henry said. He kissed her cheeks, then her lips. Amy kissed him back, and Henry felt such a swell in his heart. Strands of her wavy hair escaped her ponytail, tickling Henry's face as the kiss deepened, and then she let out the faintest of sighs.

Henry forced himself to pull back. He stood there, barely able to catch his breath, just looking at Amy in the darkness of the mist around them. She was pretty, even with the smudges of lipstick on her mouth, and her hair loose from the ponytail and mussed. As he studied her, memorizing her beauty, she moved to him and kissed him again.

Henry felt a deep stirring inside him. This girl. Amy. Her mouth on his. She was kissing him and he was trying to keep pace. They sank to the ground, until they were lying in the tall grass and Amy was on top of him.

Suddenly, for Henry this was more than some fumbling around at the school dance, or awkward necking at the movie house with some girl from school. He wanted Amy in a way he'd never wanted any girl. Wanted to possess her. Take her right there in the field, and he'd never done anything like that before, though he'd certainly thought about things like that alone in his room in the dark.

Thankfully, when Henry almost couldn't take it anymore, Amy broke away. Rolling to one side, she locked gazes with him. "This isn't . . . I mean, I shouldn't be doing this," she said, her breath ragged. "It's not right."

"I'm sorry. It's my fault," Henry said. He reached up to move a strand of Amy's hair from across her beautiful brown eyes. "But it doesn't feel wrong to me. Being with you could never feel wrong. But I'll try to be a gentleman."

"I don't want you to be," Amy said, breathlessly. "That's what I can't handle."

Henry smoothed another strand of Amy's hair. "As much as I want you, I wouldn't be pushy or try anything untoward in a field. You deserve a white wedding."

Amy let out a deep breath. "Won't be having one of those, anyway," she said softly.

Henry tried to remain calm, but his blood was racing. He shut out the mental image of Amy with anyone else—anyone but himself—and reached for her hand. "Sorry, I didn't know. That Matt character?"

Amy nodded. "There's a lot you don't know about me."

"It doesn't matter to me," he said, kissing her softly on the cheek. "Nothing you could say would make me change the way I feel about you."

"I didn't love him. I mean, I thought I did, but I don't think that's what it was." Her voice was small. "And so, white weddings aren't really—well it's not, you know, such a big deal in my time to uh, hook up with a guy."

"Hmm," Henry said. "I don't know if that's a good or bad thing."

"I wanted my first time to be special. It wasn't. Not at all," she said quietly. "So you, uh, never did it?"

"*It?*" Henry shook his head. "No."

"It's not that great," Amy said.

"If you don't love the person, I don't see how it could be," Henry said, squeezing her hand. "When you care deeply, truly, about someone, I imagine it would be wonderful." He leaned back in the grass, looking up at the whiteness that drifted across the night sky overhead.

"Yeah, I guess so," Amy said, sounding far away.

They were both quiet for a moment. Then Henry said, "If we could see the stars better, I'd look for a shooting one and make a wish."

"I don't think you need to be doing any more of that," Amy said with a small laugh.

"A wish and a prayer are like apples and oranges," Henry said. "They aren't the same thing at all."

"Yeah," Amy murmured. "Man, it really is dark. Crap." She sat up, fixing her ponytail and smoothing her dress.

"Sure, it's probably late," Henry said, raising himself to his elbows.

Amy stood up, brushing stray grass from her clothes. "I gotta go."

"When can I see you again? Promise me you'll return, Amy."

"Of course. I have a homecoming meeting after school tomorrow. So later that night, 'kay?" Amy bent down and kissed him on the cheek. And then she was gone, a distant figure vanishing in the mist.

"'Kay," Henry echoed, trying out Amy's slang, and then he lay back in the grass for a minute more, contemplating what had just happened. Amy's not saving herself for marriage didn't really bother him as much as it could have, he guessed. In her time, things were obviously different, though he did have a friend or two who'd had some experience with girls who weren't afraid of a boy making love to them. What bothered him was that Amy's first time had been with someone who didn't care about her, obviously. He would never have done that to her.

He let himself imagine Amy in his arms again, reliving each moment so he knew it had actually happened. He'd never expected to experience that kind of feeling. Love. Was that what this was? Or was it the most wonderful dream? In that case, he might as well be in heaven. And now he had to wait a whole day before he could see her again. That seemed like a lifetime.

"You've got it bad, chump," he said, shaking his head. He got up, dusted off his trousers and shirt, and walked slowly back toward the house.

As the house came into view, Henry could see his grandfather still on the porch, rocking slowly in his chair. Henry mounted the stairs, and his grandfather lifted his pipe in salute, then went back to rocking. But his gaze was on Henry.

They sat there in silence and together watched the ghostly pipe smoke twirl its way toward what Henry was beginning to see as the big, fake summer moon.

It didn't feel real anymore—nothing did without Amy.

CHAPTER FIFTEEN

I crossed the clearing and nearly skipped down the dark path through the woodlot. My heart was still pounding and my lips were warm. Henry. His name echoed in my brain, and I could smell the faintest smell of his soap on the collar of my dress. I bounded through the trees, not caring about the drizzle falling through the canopy of branches.

There was magic humming in my body—a tingling I was sure had everything to do with how I felt about Henry. My cheeks heated up when I thought about how much I'd wanted him to kiss me, how I rolled him onto the grass. I hadn't done that before— I mean, I hadn't been the one doing the rolling. It terrified and thrilled me.

I shivered in the cool night air and slowed my run as I neared the trailer. Things with Henry hadn't exactly gone as planned. There was the problem of me chickening out. *The things I hadn't said to Henry.* It wasn't exactly a mission accomplished. But I sensed he wasn't ready to hear the truth about what happened to Robert. He wasn't ready to hear that all of his efforts were for nothing. Was it so selfish to want someone to stay where they were? To stay with you forever?

I stopped at the foot of the porch stairs, feeling my exhilaration crash down to earth. Henry wasn't mine. He couldn't be. We couldn't be. There was no forever that included me. I had to tell him—tomorrow night I'd tell him.

Katie-dog was sleeping near the door, ears cocked my way as I approached.

"Hey, girl, locked out?"

She eased herself up to a standing position and wagged her tail, whining. I reached down to pet her and she was all over me, sniffing and snorting.

"Easy," I said, pushing her down.

She whined but stayed off me, and I let us into the house. I heard light snoring coming from Mae's room, which was a relief. As I got a glass of water, I glimpsed myself in the oven door's reflection—hair messed up, red lipstick smeared on my mouth. I grabbed a paper towel, dampened it in the sink, and rubbed the scarlet stain off my lips. I changed out of the dress, carefully hanging it in the closet. And then, clad in pajamas and listening to Radiohead through my earbuds, I tried to sleep.

But nothing could force Henry from my mind. Nothing.

"We really need to meet again next week?" I asked, as Jackson, Lori, and I left Mr. Planter's room the next day. "It seems like all that's left is to make the punch."

Lori gave me a pitying look. "There's so much more to it than that. I mean, no offense, Amy, but thank goodness you're not in charge." She playfully shoved my shoulder, nearly knocking me into Jackson.

"Easy," Jackson said, reaching out both hands to steady me. "Who's in for Hal's? I think we need to ponder our plan over fries."

"Yeah, my mom's making some kind of gross chili-mac casserole, so count me in," Lori said.

We reached Jackson's truck. "Amy?"

"Um, I guess," I said, glancing down at my watch.

"You guess about french fries?" Lori said as she climbed into Jackson's truck and slid over to the middle seat.

"Well, it's just that I have something later." *Something* was right.

All day, I'd been thinking about Henry, about getting back out to the clearing like I'd promised.

"That's cool if you don't want to come with," Jackson said. "Want me to run you home first?"

I hesitated long enough to see the disappointed look on Lori's face. "No," I said. Forget it. It's fine. Let's go have some fries."

"And talk about the outfits," Lori said. "This is a working dinner."

"Oh, brother," Jackson said. He threw the truck in reverse and backed out of the parking spot.

"I don't get it—are they giving out a prize for best dressed, or something? Did I miss that part of the meeting?" I said.

"No," Lori said with a sigh. "I just, well, it's stupid. Never mind."

"Okay, we will," Jackson said, winking over at me, before he pulled out of the lot and onto the road to town.

"No, we won't. C'mon, what's the deal?" I reached over and pinched Jackson.

"Ouch! Yeah, Lori, I'm sorry—I was just playing. What's so important about having the best costumes?" Jackson added.

Lori crossed her arms over her chest. "I know it probably sounds dumb, but every year, we walk into the dance and it's like we're total dorks or something. Quinn and Melanie and those people make me feel so lame."

"Um . . ." Jackson said.

"Don't make fun of me, Jackson. You totally know what I'm talking about," Lori said, her voice small.

"Well, that sucks," I said.

"Sure they're jerks, but you don't have to take it personally," Jackson said.

"Yeah, thanks. It helps to remember that when I'm crying in the bathroom stall because Melanie and her cronies laughed about my stupid dress."

"Really?" Jackson said.

Lori nodded.

After that, nobody said anything until Jackson parked the truck in an open spot at the drive-in. "I didn't know that happened," he said. "Why didn't you tell me?"

Lori sniffled and shook her head. "It was last year. I got over it."

Right. I patted Lori on the arm. "Listen, that won't happen this year. We're gonna look awesome."

"Yeah. I promise to take it more seriously," Jackson said. "Maybe we can figure out how I could get a real soldier's uniform or something."

Lori brightened. "Really?"

"Yes, really," Jackson said. He got out of the truck and waited for us to grab our stuff. Then, as Lori came around the front, he gave her a big hug.

And I couldn't help but like the two of them just a little bit more.

"That Jackson's truck out there?" Mae asked later that night.

I hung my coat up on the rack and slid out of my wet shoes. The rain had started up again. "Yeah, did you get my message? We got a hamburger after the homecoming meeting at school."

Mae clanked the door to the wood stove closed. "Yep."

"Here," I said, holding out a white paper bag. "Curly fries and a bacon burger for you."

"Well, aren't you a sweet girl? I was hoping, but I figured I'd just have a bowl of soup if worse came to worst," she said with a laugh. She took the bag from me and sat down at the table.

I plopped onto the couch and muted the detective show on TV. "So how did Jackson know you had a thing for bacon burgers?" I asked. "He insisted I get you that, but he wouldn't tell me why."

"His family may be vegetarian, but that kid worked at Hal's last summer, and let's just say that Katie-dog and I stopped by there a few times." Mae grinned at me guiltily and then slid a paper napkin onto her lap.

"I was going to get you a veggie burger—that would be a whole lot better for you, Mae. Jackson says they're really yummy."

Mae shrugged. "I'll take the bacon. Life's too short not to enjoy the good stuff," she said, and then took a big bite. Over on her dog bed near the wood stove, Katie started drooling, watching Mae eat the burger.

"So, what's on tap for tonight?" Mae said, dabbing her lips with the napkin.

"Huh?"

"You and Lori studying again? You've been spending a lot of time over there."

"Oh, um, yeah, I guess." I kept my eyes on the muted TV so I wouldn't have to fib to Mae's face. "I should go over there pretty soon." I'd told Henry I'd meet him in the clearing tonight. That was now. I wondered if he was worrying about me.

"Well, it's a nasty night to be running down to her place. You want a ride?"

"Nah, I'll bundle up." I left Mae to her burger and went to my room. I took the solid blue dress out of the closet and laid it on the bed. I took off my jeans and hoodie and pulled the dress on. I shimmied the dress down around my hips and then reached around to zip myself up.

"Need any help?"

I froze as Mae came in. Behind me in the mirror's reflection, she appraised me. "Hmm, blue suits you."

"It's for the dance," I said. "You know, homecoming."

Mae sat down on my bed. "And this is your idea of bundling

up? Amy, it's pouring rain outside. How are you going to walk a quarter mile in that?"

"Wearing a coat," I said.

Mae let out a sigh. "Sweetie—sit down."

I didn't like the tone in her voice. "Mae, why are you making such a big deal out of this?" I walked to the mirror and reached for the pins on my dresser to pin back my curls in waves.

"What is . . . *this?*" Mae said, gesturing toward me and my outfit. "That's all I'm trying to find out."

"This is—just dress up." I grabbed a red lipstick and dabbed a little on my lower lip. I could feel Mae's eyes on me, but I didn't turn around.

"Amy, come on. Have a seat," Mae said, patting the bed. "Let's you and I have a talk for a minute."

I sat down across from her.

"I'm not one to check up on you, but I saw Lori's mom at the grocery store today and I thanked her for letting you come by so often to visit. She didn't know what I was talking about."

My heart sank. "Oh."

"*Oh* is right. You weren't going over to Lori's tonight, were you?" When Mae looked at me that way, her blue eyes stony and her mouth grim, there was no way I could keep lying.

"Okay, no. I'm not going to Lori's."

Mae let out a sigh of disappointment. "Amy, the first rule was that we were going to tell each other the truth—even if it was hard. Remember?"

"Yeah." My cheeks flushed with shame. "I'm sorry."

"Now, I don't mean to threaten you—I love having you here with me—but if this lying keeps up, well, your mom and Pete are moving to Arizona in just under a month. There's still time to send you with them," Mae said. "So, will you tell your old auntie what's going on out there?"

My heart stilled. "Out *there?*"

"Out there in the fog. That's where you're headed again, right?"

I didn't say anything for a moment. I stared down at my dress, examining the fine stitching, the pretty buttons. "Truthfully— yes," I said.

"What on earth has you running out to the back pasture in the dark?"

"You're not going to believe me, Mae."

"Try me. I think I've heard most everything by this point in my life, sweetie," Mae said. "Whatever it is—if it's just some boy you're meeting or even UFOs landing, I'd like you to simply tell me the truth."

I winced at the mention of boys—of course Mae would think I had fallen into another crappy relationship with a boy who treated me like dirt. How could I ever explain to her the way I felt when I was with Henry, how different he was from anyone I'd ever met, or ever cared about?

"Amy, I'm getting older by the second. Out with it," Mae said, sounding a bit exasperated.

"I can't believe I'm going to say this—and I don't think you're going to believe me—but whatever. Henry Briggs and his family are in the back field."

"The Briggses?"

I nodded. "It sounds dumb and made up, but the family is real. So real. It's Henry and his mother and his grandfather. They're real and really there."

Mae let out a long sigh. "I don't know what to say. You know on TV, the ghost hunters use all kinds of equipment; they don't dress up in costume," she said, eyeballing my dress.

"They aren't ghosts, not really," I said. "They're from another time. They're living in the past because the past never went forward."

"This is pretty out there, kiddo."

"You think I'm lying," I said, letting out a sigh. "And I did lie about Lori's, but how could I tell you I've been going out to the field to see people who shouldn't be there?"

"You're going to visit a ghost—and here I worried about your sneaking out to see live boys," Mae said, shaking her head.

"Henry *is* alive, Mae. He's in 1944, but he's alive."

"I don't know how that's possible," she said.

"They didn't die—they disappeared into a pocket of time," I said, trying to break it down for her. "Henry prayed for the end of summer never to come, and it didn't."

"Why did he do that?"

"I'm pretty sure he thinks his brother Robert died, but I saw in the newspaper he didn't. He was found in a prisoner of war camp and lived to be an old man." I reached into my pocket and pulled out the obituary I'd printed at the library the day before.

Mae took the paper from me and read it. "Well, I knew Robert didn't die. He sold my daddy the property after the war. He sold it because his family had disappeared. They had abandoned that house and were never heard from again."

"They disappeared into a pocket of time. That's what I'm trying to tell you."

"And they never knew that Robert lived?"

"No, and they still don't. And I thought Henry and his family would want to know, but I couldn't tell him the other night. There's something else—something else that happened to them after that. Henry seemed really upset about it the other night, so I didn't get a chance to tell him about Robert. Those boys from the past, they aren't the world's biggest talkers."

Mae looked at me intently. "They are very real to you, aren't they?"

"They'd be real to you, too, Mae. If you only met them, you'd get it. Seriously. What can I do to convince you they're real? Do you want to come with me?"

Mae blinked at me. "On a night like this? Heavens no."

"Well, look—I promised Henry I'd come see him tonight. I'm only going over there for a little while. I'm sorry. I know I shouldn't have lied about it, Mae, but I have to see him tonight. I have to tell him what I found out."

Mae wiped a hand across her forehead. "This is a lot to take in, Amy."

"So you believe me?"

"Yes and no." She got up from the bed. "But listen—I don't like your going out in the dark alone. I can't go chasing you down if you get lost out there."

"You want me to be honest, right? Well, I'm going out there whether you believe me or not—whether you want me to or not."

She looked at me, a mixture of weariness and acceptance in her eyes. "I don't expect I'd be able to stop you."

"And I don't want to lie," I said. "I'm going now. I'm not going to get lost." I hugged Mae, ignoring the fact that she was stiff in my arms. "I promise I'll be careful."

"I don't like this. You be back soon," she said, releasing me from the hug. "And never, ever lie to me again."

"I won't need to," I said. I followed her out into the living room and put on my heavy coat and boots. I stuffed some flip-flops into my pockets.

"And for goodness' sake, these ghosts—these . . . whatever you think you saw—tell them everything. If that's why they're hanging around, you can release them. They should know the truth."

"Yeah, I know," I said, heading to the back door. "I know."

I crossed into the clearing, shed my raincoat and boots near the stump, and threw on the flip-flops. As I passed into Henry's world, I breathed in the warm summer breeze that greeted me, trying to calm myself. I was excited and more than a little nervous as I started down the path toward the farmhouse.

But something was different.

In the twilight blue, the house seemed like a beacon of white light. The last time I'd been there, Henry and his grandfather had been lounging on the front porch. Tonight, their seats were empty, and light, instead of radio tunes, flooded out from the windows.

I mounted the stairs, almost afraid to call out a hello. And then I heard low voices. I stopped at the back door, peering through the window into the kitchen. Henry and his grandpa were sitting at the table, cups of coffee in their hands.

I raised my hand to knock just as Henry looked up and saw me. His face was pained. He shook his head and I dropped my hands to my side. He didn't want me knocking, for some reason. Okay.

Henry got up from the table, said something to his grandpa, and then came to the back door. He opened it slowly, quietly, and said, "Hello, Amy."

"Hi, what's the deal?"

He let himself through the door and came out onto the porch. "My mother's having a bad time tonight. She's taken ill," he said.

"What's wrong—is there anything I can do?"

"Thank you for offering, but I don't think so."

I sat down on the porch swing, but he didn't sit next to me.

"This isn't the best time for us to visit," he said in a quiet voice. "Why don't you let me walk you to the clearing?"

I almost lost my nerve, almost took the easy way out again. "No, I have to talk to you tonight. It's important."

"Amy," Henry said, "another time."

I felt a tightness in my throat. "No, I can't put this off. I thought about it a lot and we really have to talk, okay?"

"Amy," Henry said, "my mother's problem is bigger than just a headache."

"Okay, fine," I said. "What's going on?"

Henry glanced back toward the kitchen window and then sat down next to me on the swing bench. "She tried to leave the farm today."

"Oh." I waited for Henry to say more.

"I talked her out of walking down to church on Sunday, but today, my mother got the idea of taking the neighbors some of our extra honey. She wandered into the fog at the end of the road and got confused and scared. It came time for dinner and I couldn't find her, so I went looking. She was down by the creek, crying. She'd been there for hours."

"What did she think happened?"

"I don't know. She hasn't said a word since I found her. Look, Amy, things are changing. She'd never tried to leave the farm before. Not once since this endless summer began."

"Why are things changing?" I asked, dreading the answer.

Henry looked up at me, concern in his eyes. "You're the only thing different," he said. "Before you came along, things were the same. They were boring, but they were the same."

I let out a breath. "And now your grandpa is asking questions, and your mom is wanting to go places . . ."

He nodded. "Pandora's box."

"But is that such a bad thing? That they want to really live? That they might want things to be different, to be more normal?"

Henry's jaw tightened. "It's not good."

"And you're blaming all that on me," I said, slowly. "So you don't think *any* of this is good." I shook my head.

"Now hold on," he said. "You're the only good thing that's happened to me in forever. You know that." He leaned over and kissed me gently.

I pulled back from his lips. "Yeah, I guess, but don't blame me for showing up and ruining your perfect life, okay?"

Henry reached for my hand. "There are things going on here

that you don't know about. Things I haven't told you. I have no right to burden you with my troubles. You've got enough of your own."

"Well, sometimes you have to share what's on your mind." I paused, gathering my courage. "Henry, I did come here tonight to get to the truth with you. So can we do that? Then I'll leave you alone to deal with your family."

Henry nodded.

I took a deep breath and prepared to tell him what I knew. But Henry spoke first.

CHAPTER SIXTEEN

"You know my mother is not well." He didn't want to sound like a complainer. He didn't want Amy to feel sorry for him, or to judge him for what he'd done. But if she was going to understand what was happening, how being with her, as beautiful as it had been, was affecting the family, then he had to tell it to her straight. He turned on the bench so he was looking directly into Amy's eyes.

"She's been feeling poorly since my father died a while back." His voice was quiet. "And then Robert shipped out to the army a year and a half ago and she got worse."

"It's natural to get depressed when someone has a loss," Amy said. "All the doctors say that."

"Well, her doctor's a quack," he said.

"He didn't give her any help?"

"Oh, he helped her all right—helped her with some pills," Henry said, barely able to keep the anger from his voice.

"Lots of people are on medication for depression," Amy said. "It's something that people get treated for in my time."

"Well, this doctor's treatment didn't help. It hurt." He looked away, unable to take Amy's concerned stare. "It was a hot June day and I'd just made it home from swimming with my chums down at the river. Mother had made fried chicken, a special treat. We were sitting down to eat supper and there was a knock at the door. Mother answered, and then I heard her screaming. I ran out to see what was happening and saw the telegram in her hand. I felt so guilty. We'd had a first telegram ten days before—one that said Robert was missing in action after the invasion at Normandy.

The infantry had landed at Omaha Beach on the sixth and no one had seen him since. I'd *hid* that telegram, Amy. I'd hid that one because I knew what she'd do. I just knew. But I hadn't thought about when this one would come. And this one said Robert was presumed dead. It was so much worse."

"But, Robert was—"

"Please." Henry held up a hand. "Let me finish my story." He forced breath into his lungs, then made himself struggle onward. "My mother took to her room. She wouldn't come out, no matter what Grandpa or I said. She cried all night and in the morning"— he took another deep breath—"in the morning, Grandpa and I found her unconscious—the pill bottle empty on her nightstand. I fetched the doctor from town, but he said Mother was coma-tose. She wouldn't wake up, Amy. I prayed that night—I prayed that we'd never got the telegram, that everything was like it was before. And darned if it didn't come true. The very next day, the summer started over. The prayer erased away what had happened to us like whitewash over a dirty wall. We began again."

"You poor mother," Amy said.

Henry stiffened. He'd often felt sorry for his mother in her grief, but since that night, anger mixed with his pity. How ready she'd been to just leave him behind, how ready just to give up. "It was hard for all of us."

Amy was watching him. "Henry, what if Robert wasn't killed?" she said in a tentative tone.

"That's what I prayed about," Henry said.

"No, you prayed for the telegram not to come, but what if your brother was alive? Wouldn't your mother be okay? I mean, there'd be no reason to try to hurt herself, right?" Amy's eyes looked luminous in the porch light. She was so hopeful, so naive.

"Are you're saying I prayed for the wrong miracle?"

She shook her head. "I need to tell you something. I think it's going to be hard for you to take—but listen—Robert didn't die in the war. That's what I wanted to tell you the other night, but I couldn't."

Henry's mind whirled. "What are you saying?"

"I don't know if it's right to tell you about what happens in the future—your future that is, or what—but I know Robert survived," Amy said. "Seriously, Henry."

He closed his eyes. "How do you know Robert survived?" he said, barely able to form the words.

"I found it in an old newspaper article. At Normandy, he was captured by the German army. He wasn't killed. He lived to be an old man. Look!" She thrust a piece of paper at Henry.

Henry didn't take the paper from Amy. He couldn't look at it. He didn't know what to think—whether to be happy or to be angry. He thought of his brother walking up the drive, his duffle bag on his shoulder, and his mother running to meet him with tears streaming down her face. He thought of fishing at the creek with Robert, of talking with him about life and girls. Of hiking up to the old mine and hunting for soapstone to carve. There were so many things he missed about his brother. Joy and loneliness flooded him. And fear. Still the fear.

"I wish you hadn't told me this," Henry said, after a moment.

Amy's face reddened and she set the paper between them on the bench. "Why wouldn't you want to know that your brother didn't die?" she said, matching his angry tone.

"So Robert lives. Does that mean my mother doesn't take the pills when she gets the telegram?" Henry said. "Does that mean she doesn't die?"

"You don't know that she dies! You know that she slipped into a coma. That's not the same thing, Henry. And what if you told her the telegram was a mistake? What if you told her that Robert is alive?"

"And expect her to believe that the U.S. government was

wrong? Why would she believe me? She would be heading for that jar of pills just the same. You don't know how she is."

"So, maybe she won't believe you at first, but maybe it gives her hope. Hope enough to hang on until the army finds out its mistake and Robert comes home to her, to all of you."

"Hope left her long ago," he said.

"And did it leave you, too?"

Henry got up from the bench and went to lean on the railing of the porch.

Amy followed, taking a place beside him. "Don't you think you deserve to live more of a life than just this summer?"

"Amy, I can't take the chance that Mother will hurt herself."

"And that you'll go into the service," she replied softly. "If time goes forward, you'll be off to war like Robert."

Henry's heart stilled. "What's that got to do with it? You want me to ship out?"

"No, of course not! Mae lost her love, Joe Hansen, in the war. She's still sad after all these years. You think I want that? To lose you like she lost her Joe and never love again?"

"I don't know anything about Joe Hansen and your auntie. Why are you—well—what's the big idea with all of this, anyway? I thought you cared about me, and now you're telling me to move on. The other night, you told me you didn't want me to go."

Amy's eyes darkened. "There's no *big idea*. I thought you needed to know that Robert was alive. Since I found out, I felt dishonest carrying that truth around. When you care about someone, you don't lie to them. That's not love."

"You know all about that, huh?" he said, in a harsher tone than he meant.

What was left of her composure crumbled.

The sight of tears welling in Amy's eyes made Henry feel like a heel. "Look, can't you just let me alone now?" he said. "You told me what you had to get off your chest, and now you're free." He turned away, unable to look at her anymore. He didn't want to think about what she'd told him, how she wanted him to go on without her.

"I thought you'd want to know," Amy repeated, her words ragged.

Henry let out a deep breath. "It doesn't change anything for me. Not a thing."

"But it could," Amy said. "Your mother deserves to know he's okay."

"I'm not going to let anything happen to her, to this," he said, gesturing to the farm. "You go on home." Coldness crept into his voice, and he hated himself for it.

"Look, Henry, will you at least understand that I'm not telling you this because I want you to leave me," Amy said, moving toward the porch stairs. "I had to tell you."

"Go on to your sunny, bright future," Henry said in a quiet voice. "I won't be there." He didn't look up, but he heard Amy sobbing as she ran down the porch and into the night. Her sudden absence was like a slap in the face, and Henry took it gladly.

He knew in his heart he deserved it.

His coffee was cold when Henry returned to his place at the kitchen table.

"What'd you do to that sweet girl to make her run off like that?" Grandpa said, setting down his cup.

"Nothing," Henry said. The lie flushed his cheeks.

"Hogwash."

Henry kept his eyes on his coffee cup. "All right, she's sore at me. It's not a mountain, it's a molehill," he said.

"That girl cares for you," Grandpa said. "I didn't raise you to be callous."

"I wasn't being callous. We've had a misunderstanding, that's all." He took a sip of coffee, hoping that was the end of the conversation. But Grandpa kept on.

"Son, I haven't seen you that starry-eyed over a girl in ages. Why would you treat your sweetheart that way?"

"She's not my sweetheart," Henry said, adding *anymore* in his mind.

"Hogwash," Grandpa said again. "You love that girl, and she's fool enough to love you back."

Henry glanced up at Grandpa, considering his words. Maybe he did love Amy. Maybe that's why this hurt so darn bad. The thought of never seeing her again burned an angry fire inside of him. "Well, she's through with me," he muttered.

"Son, I heard some of what the girl said."

Henry swallowed another sip of coffee, avoiding his grandfather's stare.

"Were you fighting about your brother? She said something about him. How does she know your brother?"

"Amy doesn't know Robert. She just thinks she does," Henry said. He rubbed the back of his neck, trying to ease the headache he felt forming.

"I heard her say he's alive," Grandpa said, his eyebrows drawing together. "What would she mean by that?"

"She's making conversation. Of course he's alive," Henry replied.

"Actually, we don't know that," Grandpa said. "We don't know anything for certain about the operation over there. The men and even some of the women nurses lose their lives every day. That's the evil of war, son. It costs human lives."

"As far as I'm concerned, he's alive and well and fighting alongside the other brave men." Henry's voice was icy.

"Why are you talking about your brother?" Mother stood in the doorway, dressed in her pink dressing gown. Her eyes were red and bloodshot, her hands shaky as she steadied herself against the jamb. "Has something happened?"

"No, Mother," Henry said. "Come have a seat."

"Thank you, no. I'll stand," she said.

"Don't be silly, Alma. Take a chair," Grandpa said, getting up and escorting her to the table. "Let me get you a drink of water."

Henry and his mother sat in silence, looking at each other across the table for a moment, and then Grandpa returned with the glass. Mother took it from Grandpa and paused. Henry watched her pat her robe pocket, probably searching for her pill bottle. She came up with a handkerchief and Henry relaxed in his chair.

Mother wiped her eyes and then drank some of the water. "I want to know what is happening to us," she said, turning to Henry. "I want to know why I can't go down the road. I want to know why we always seem to have enough to eat, but I never ride into town for supplies. I want to know why I never get any letters from Robert—or anyone else, for that matter. It's as if I've been sleepwalking through life. The more I thought about it, sitting in the quiet by myself today, the more I started to wonder about all these peculiar things, Henry. Can you explain it to me? Or am I going as plum crazy as I feel?"

Grandpa took his seat at the table. "You're not crazy, Alma. Sometimes, I swear I must be doing the same thing every day. I know every checker move Henry ever played. Everything seems familiar, from the way my carrots grow in the garden, to the direction my pipe smoke curls every night."

Henry felt panic rising inside him and a sick, strange feeling starting in his stomach.

"Will you please help us understand?" Mother asked. "I want to know, son. I need to know the truth. You seem to be the only one who knows what that is."

CHAPTER SEVENTEEN

Without meaning to, I slammed the back door of the trailer. The theme of the nightly news show was playing loudly from the living room. I jammed my heavy coat onto the rack and kicked off my boots. Rain dripped from my hair down the back of my neck, and my dress felt heavy on my skin. I had to get out of it. Wanted to rip the pins from my hair and smear this damn lipstick off my mouth.

Katie whined from her dog bed, then got up and ran over to me, sniffing.

"Down, girl," I said, pushing her off me. "Leave me alone."

Mae woke from her deep sleep in her recliner. "What? What's happening?"

"Nothing," I lied, breaking the promise I'd made to Mae only hours before. I went to the bathroom and plucked out tissues. I squished makeup remover on them, rubbed the scarlet stain from my lips, and then went to work on my mascara. It was halfway down my face, anyway—half from the rain and half from Henry. He didn't want me there. Hadn't been glad I'd told him about Robert. Hadn't done anything I expected.

I wet a washcloth and scrubbed my face, trying to keep from crying more over some dumb guy from decades ago. I patted dry with a towel and then pulled the pins from my hair, dropping them into the drawer one by one. In my room, I stepped out of the dress, leaving it in a circle on the floor. It was good to throw on a T-shirt and sweatpants, and when I appraised myself in the mirror, blotchy face, reddened eyes, and hair hanging down like normal, I felt better.

Here was the real me. I wasn't some girl in 1944. I was just me in a trailer now. And that was all I was. I didn't have a boyfriend from the past. I didn't have anyone who could hurt me. Anyone who could make me believe it was okay to trust them and then throw me away.

"Sweetie, what's going on?" Mae said from her chair as I came back into the living room.

"I'm done with the clearing," I said.

"You're done with the ghost of Henry Briggs?" she said with a knowing look.

"He's not a . . . oh, never mind," I said. I went into the kitchen and fired up the teakettle. Maybe he was just a ghost. Maybe that was truly why he didn't want to cross over to my side or even finish living his own life. Weren't you a ghost if you were afraid to move on?

Mae lumbered into the kitchen. "You want to talk about it?" she asked.

I rummaged in the cabinet for tea. "No, Mae. I don't think so."

"You say that, but I don't believe you. Talk to me."

I looked at her sitting there at the table. It was like seeing her for the first time. This big, gray old woman who was willing to believe my crazy story about ghosts in the back field. This lady who had taken me in and done her best to give me space. This aunt who talked more with me than my own mother had. Or at least she tried to talk with me, when I wasn't running off to chase some fantasy in the mist.

"Oh, sweetie," she said.

Tears streamed down my face. "He sent me away," I said. "He didn't want to hear the truth, and he sent me away."

"Come here," Mae said. She stood up and opened her arms. "Come here, baby."

I let her hug me. I let her hold me while I cried. We both

ignored the whistling teakettle until Katie started barking at the noise.

Mae sat me down in a chair and went to make the tea. "I'm so sorry you had to go through that," she said a moment later, setting a cup in front of me.

I swiped at my eyes with the sleeves of my sweatshirt.

"Now then, tea makes everything better, remember?" Mae said.

And then she sat there with me, sipping from her cup of chamomile while I told her everything. Everything about stupid Matt Parker. Everything about stupid Henry Briggs.

She didn't say anything. She just let me talk. And when I'd cried for, like, the tenth time—when I was all cried out—she hugged me again and kissed me on the head.

"No boy ever makes you special. You just are." She pulled away from the hug to look me in the eyes. "Understand?"

I nodded. I wasn't sure I did understand. But I felt so much love for Mae in that moment, it was a good lie.

A week went by. I didn't go beyond the woodlot. Though I could see it, I avoided the misty field. I went to school. I did my homework. I tried to look forward to the dance. As Mae reminded me, this day was all I had. Each day was all anyone ever had for sure, so I had to enjoy it. I forced myself at first.

I tried not to think about Henry. Tried not to see his handsome face when I closed my eyes. Tried not to imagine his arms wrapped around me. It just made me sad.

And then I decided I had to make forgetting about Henry easier. So one day after school, I took Katie-dog for a walk down the outer road Mae had told me about. Sure enough, we never came to the mist-filled clearing going this way. We wandered down the potholed, graveled lane for half a mile or so and then came to an overgrown driveway—the forgotten entrance to the farmhouse Mae's father had bought from Robert Briggs.

I walked in the tire ruts, flanked by overgrown grass, with Katie whining as she trotted alongside me. Just beyond some withered hydrangea bushes, stacks of blackened bricks still held the rough shape of a crumbled chimney. The rain stung my cheeks as I pulled back my hood to take a better look. Flagstones and charred wood were heaped in small piles, remnants of the fire that had happened years ago. Just as I had seen in Mae's old photograph, Henry's beautiful farmhouse lay in ruins.

As if on autopilot, I walked to the backyard, to the apple tree I'd stood beneath with Henry so many times. Instead of the lovely fruit-filled beacon of Henry's world, I found a twisted, old tree, lonely and hunched against the rain. Crushed, rotting fruit littered the ground, squishing under my boots. My eyes filled with tears as I pulled Henry's monogrammed handkerchief from my pocket and tied it to one of the gnarled, leafless branches.

"C'mon, Katie-dog. There's nothing for us here." I made my way through the decomposing apples to the path but couldn't resist a last look over my shoulder at the tree. The hankie stood out like a white flag of surrender on a dark, mossy landscape.

Fighting another wave of sadness, I hurried down the overgrown driveway. I wish I could say it didn't hurt to see what the magical farm had become, what the reality of Henry's world really was. But it did hurt.

And it felt like the hurt was necessary.

About a week later, when thoughts of Henry crossed my mind, I told myself he'd probably forgotten all about me. Another week passed, and I told myself I was a distant memory to him, a summer day that had flashed by like so many before, so long ago that he maybe even wondered if I'd ever happened.

And I'd become the ghost. Only I'd disappeared forever.

"Oh dear, he'll be here any minute. I want to get some pictures before you go." Mae shuffled slowly out of my room, leaving me to finish pinning my hair that Friday night.

I pursed my lips and applied a layer of red to top off the look. Stepping back from the mirror, I scratched the back of one of my ankles with the opposite foot. Though Mae's old pumps were slightly big, I was standing taller—and feeling all right, considering. It felt odd to have the burgundy dress on again, the dress I'd been wearing when Henry had kissed me for the first time. It felt heavy on my skin, like it was carrying the weight of my broken heart. But I was over that now. It was just another dress. And this was just another dance.

"The forties look really suits you," Mae said, coming back into the room. She was breathing heavily with the effort of hurrying. "But, sweetie, you need some jewelry. I want you to try these pearls." She held out a box containing a beautiful necklace and matching earrings.

"Mae, sit down and rest, okay? You've really been pushing yourself today," I said.

"Aw, not more than usual," she said, taking a place on the edge of my bed. "All righty, let's see them on."

"'Kay." I fastened the necklace around my neck, and then I slipped on the matching clip-on earrings. The pearls shone brilliantly in the light. I had to admit they looked great. "What do you think?"

"I think they're yours," Mae said with a smile. "I want you to have them."

"Oh, Mae. You don't have to give them to me. I'll just borrow them."

"No, no. I've enjoyed them for many years, but I think it's time I handed them down to you. They were a gift from my father."

"Thank you." I gave Mae a big hug and reappraised myself in the mirror. With the pearls, the dark red dress looked just right. I couldn't help thinking that Henry would have loved to see this— me all done up in 1940s clothes for the last time.

"You look so beautiful." Mae gave a wistful sigh as she clicked a photo. "I'm going to send these snapshots to your mom and Pete. They'll be thrilled to see you all dressed up and happy."

Happy? I didn't correct Mae. I just gave my hair a last pat and checked my teeth for lipstick.

Mae raised herself to her feet and came over to stand behind me in the mirror. "I hear Jackson's truck in the driveway. You're going to have a lovely time with him."

"Yeah," I said, but my voice must have betrayed my doubts.

Mae smiled at me in the mirror. "Come on now. None of that, sweetie. He's a good kid."

"I'd rather just stay home with you," I said.

"Stay home with an old woman instead of having fun at the dance? You might as well enjoy being young."

I turned to reply and she snapped another photo. "Geez, Mae!" I went to let Jackson in, the flash still blinding me.

I opened the door and sucked in a breath. Jackson stood on the doorstep, an uncertain look in his eyes and a corsage in his hands. His vintage U.S. Navy outfit was dazzling white. "Hi," I said.

"Hey." His gaze raked over me from head to toe, but his expression didn't change. I crossed my arms over my chest and itched the back of my calf with the opposite foot again.

"Amy," Jackson said, "I—I don't know what to say. You're breathtaking."

I blotted my lips together. "Um, thanks."

"Oh, who is this charming sailor on leave?" Mae said, clapping her hands together as she approached behind me. "You look wonderful!"

"Be careful or she'll blind you with the flash." I pulled him inside and shut the door.

Mae retreated slowly to her recliner, the camera ready in her hands. Katie sniffed Jackson once, then trotted over to her bed by the wood stove.

"So, we should go. You ready?" I said.

Jackson's cheeks went deep pink as he looked down at the box in his hands. "These are yours. From me. Gardenias. They smell nice."

"Why are you talking like Frankenstein?"

"Sorry, sorry. I'm an idiot," he said, fumbling to open the corsage box.

The camera flashed.

"Mae, do you mind?"

A devilish grin on her face, Mae winked from the recliner.

"I, uh, well, should I put these on you?" he said, reaching forward to pin the white flowers on my dress.

"Here." I took his hands and guided him, and we got the corsage pinned on. The deep sweetness of the flowers drifted up. "They're nice. Thanks," I said.

"They look good against the red," he said. "And the red looks stunning on you."

I shifted on my feet. "So, um, should we go?"

"Wait! Wait!" Mae raised herself out of her chair and started clicking away. "Oh, you do make a gorgeous couple."

I coughed and gave Mae a look, while Jackson blushed deeply again.

"We're going in a group," I said, repeating the information for the hundredth time to Mae.

"Just friends," Jackson said with a sad shrug.

I let him help me on with my wrap, and we headed out into the rain.

We met up with Lori, Mindy, and Jackson's cousin, Rob, in the parking lot of the Cascades Inn, one of the only two restaurants in town. Everybody had made an effort to dress the part of characters in *Pearl Harbor*. Lori had on a retro-looking pink dress with a jacket and white gloves, and Mindy wore a blue satin dress with a full skirt. Rob was wearing a plain gray suit with a tie, but his fedora hat gave him a forties feel.

When we went inside, we all learned that not only had Jackson called ahead to make a reservation, but his aunt Barb, who worked there, had arranged a special table for us. We breezed ahead of the line of couples waiting—including Quinn and Melanie—and followed Barb to a big round table underneath a wagon wheel chandelier. She gave us an approving nod and went to get our waters.

I studied the laminated menu, while Lori and Mindy chatted away.

"And look at Mia and Chris—they must be doing *Twilight*," Lori said.

"He looks like the undead, all right."

I glanced from table to table, noticing that we were the only group in the room. Every other spot was filled with couples going to the dance and old people having dinner and gazing into each other's eyes.

Suddenly, I wanted that. I wanted to be with someone who truly loved me. I didn't understand why that had to be so difficult. First, Matt Parker had broken my heart. Now there was Henry, a boy who didn't even exist and yet had rejected me all the same —and just for telling the truth. Maybe everything I'd thought was love up to this point was as fake as Henry's eternal summer.

"Everything okay?" whispered Jackson, holding up his opened menu in front of us like a screen.

"Yeah, fine."

He gave me a look like he didn't believe me. "Sure?"

I shrugged and said, "It's just weird being out."

"With the whole town watching, you mean," Jackson said, adding a little wink. "Don't worry. You'll be fine."

I dredged up a smile for him. This was a night to have fun and I was going to have to stop thinking about stupid boy stuff. "It is a little unnerving, but you're right," I said. "I'll be fine."

Jackson lowered the menu back to the table and said, "I'd suggest the eggplant parm."

"What?"

"For dinner. The eggplant parmesan?" he repeated. "It's pretty good."

Across the table, Lori and Mindy had gone quiet and were watching us.

I relaxed and smoothed my napkin on my lap. "Yeah, I guess we should figure out what we're ordering, huh?"

"Yep. You check it out, and I'll be right back," Jackson said. He got up from the table and headed down the hall to the restroom. Meanwhile, Rob wandered away from us girls to chat with a friend at another table.

"Ohmigosh, are you guys cute or what?" said Lori, leaning over.

"Uh-huh." I scanned the menu, trying to let go of everything churning around in my mind.

"I don't get it," said Mindy in an annoyed voice. "Is no one in our town good enough for you?"

I set down the menu. "What do you mean by that?"

"You don't like Jackson. You never hang out. You'd rather stay cooped up in that tiny trailer with your old aunt. People wonder," Mindy said with a shrug.

I scanned her face to see if she was freaking serious. "Mindy, this is the first time you and I have ever hung out. Seriously, you're in my Creative Living class. Does that make you an expert on me? You don't even know who I am."

"Of course I don't. You never took the chance to let anyone get to know you," said Mindy.

"That's rid—"

"Amy!" Lori held up a hand. "Mindy has a point. I mean, aside from me and Jackson, you haven't really met anyone else."

"Exactly," Mindy said.

"Ouch," I muttered. "Well, with friends like you . . ."

"Amy, it's sorta true, isn't it?" Lori said, her voice softening. "It's like you haven't really given this town a chance. And you're sure not giving Jackson one, either."

"If he's so great, then you date him," I said, putting my napkin on my plate.

"I would—but he only likes one girl," Lori said with a wistful smile. "And it's breaking his heart because it's a total waste of his time."

Without a word, I grabbed my purse and wrap and walked off. I brushed past Jackson on his return to the table. "Hey, what's— hey, where're you going?"

"I'm getting some air," I said. I stalked past the revolving dessert display, ignoring the stares of the kids waiting in line for tables.

At the edge of the building, I found a dark corner out of the rain. I fished my cell from my purse and held it in my hands for a minute. I meant to dial Mae, to ask her to come get me. But another phone number flashed in my brain and by rote, I started dialing.

The voice on the other end of the line was gruff. "Hey? Who is this? You're not in my phone."

"Matt?" I said weakly.

"Babe? Is that you?" He sounded excited, maybe even happy.

My heart soared. "Yeah."

"That your new number? Your stupid mom wouldn't give it to me," he said, adding a dry-sounding laugh.

"Yeah. It's my new cell."

It got quiet, and I could hear Matt's breathing and the drizzling of rain on the pavement beyond my corner. Headlights from a car speeding down the highway lit up my corner for a few seconds and then plunged me into darkness again where the road turned.

"So," he said, "I missed you."

"What about Chelsea?" I asked.

"What about her? We broke up at the end of the summer."

"Yeah?"

"Uh-huh. It wasn't working out. So, where are you? I tried to find out, but your mom wouldn't say. She always did hate me," he said.

"Not always."

"Hmm. I want to see you. I miss you," he said, his voice low and rumbly.

Warmth rushed into my chest. "I—I missed you, too," I said. And it came out so easily, it didn't even feel like I was lying. In fact, I'm not sure that I was.

"Where are you?"

I swallowed back the lump in my throat. "Rockville. I'm staying with my great-aunt Mae in this dump of a town."

"Nice," he said. "Country girl, yee-haw."

I smiled. I could picture him making a goofy face at me like he did sometimes.

"You gonna be down to visit your mom anytime soon?" he asked.

"I don't know," I said.

"I'd take you out to dinner. I'd even make you dinner," he said. "In fact, my parents are heading out of town on vacation soon. Maybe you could come down. I can think of lots of things we could do with the house to ourselves," he said.

"Um. I don't know."

"Tsk, tsk," he said, the seduction suddenly gone from his voice. "Same old tease, Amy, huh? Thought maybe you'd changed."

"What?"

"Come on, you know what I mean. Always teasing, and never, well, *almost never* giving it up," he said, exhaling.

"Don't you want to just hang out? I mean, you said you missed me."

The line went quiet. "I say a lot of things," he said finally.

And then I heard a click.

"What? No freaking way!" I clicked my phone off and stuffed it back into my purse. I willed myself not to cry, but the tears came anyway. Leaning against the building, I stared out at the rain as another car's headlights blazed over me, then faded away. Stupid Matt. Stupid me. I was mad at myself for calling him. And even madder at myself for believing he actually missed me. I wrapped my arms around my chest, trying to warm myself.

"Hey! You want my jacket?" Jackson walked toward me. "It's freezing out here," he said.

"No. Thanks, anyway." I sniffed and wiped my cheeks.

"You want to come back inside?" he offered.

"Not really, but I will," I said.

He cracked a smile. "Whatever they said, I'm sure they're really sorry about it," Jackson said. "You know how mean girls can be."

I shrugged. I didn't care about Lori and her friend. I didn't care about anything. None of this was real. And apparently, none of my old life was real, either.

Somehow, I made it through the rest of dinner. I didn't really talk to Lori and Mindy, though they apologized profusely. I mean, maybe they were right—maybe I hadn't really given the town a chance, and actually I didn't care that I hadn't. The only good thing about the town, well, except for Jackson, was Henry. *Had been* Henry.

When we reached the school parking lot, Jackson opened the truck door and helped me out. He hadn't said much on the way over, and I was grateful for that. He held an umbrella over my head as I teetered across the pavement in my heels. Lori, Rob, and Mindy were just ahead of us in line to enter.

Inside, the gym was all decked out for the dance. The balloons Lori and I had blown up earlier that day were tacked up everywhere. The red carpet was rolled out, and couples were posing in front of a backdrop of the Hollywood sign for their official homecoming photos. Rob and Jackson went off to hang up our coats and umbrellas. Mindy pushed ahead through the crowd, but I nearly ran right into Lori, who'd paused on the carpet. Clearly terrified, she was staring straight ahead at Melanie and her entourage.

In that moment, I seriously felt for Lori. I knew what it was like to be *that* girl. To have fear take you over so completely, you'd rather freeze in one place than go forward and fail again spectacularly. I wasn't going to let her fail. "Hey. You look great," I said, putting an arm around her shoulders. "Let's walk in there and give them something to talk about."

Lori reached down to smooth her skirt. "You sure? I don't have lipstick on my teeth? Cat hair on my wrap?"

"No. Don't you worry about those idiots, okay?"

She gave me a grateful smile.

I turned to go, but she put a hand on my arm. "Hey, Amy— wait. I'm sorry about before at the restaurant. You know me, I always talk way too much. I should have shut me and Mindy both up."

"No, it's okay," I said. "It was probably true."

She sighed. "Well, I want you to know, you are a good friend. I really mean it." Her face looked so serious, her brown eyes searching my face for a reaction.

"Aw, thanks, Lori." I hugged her. "You ready? Let's do this," I said.

"Yeah." Lori threw back her shoulders, strutting down the red carpet toward the photographers. She grabbed Rob's hand and pulled him into line with her, along with Mindy.

"Whew! What's got into Lori?" Jackson said, returning from the coat check.

"Nothing."

Jackson smiled. "Well, I'm glad you two worked it out. She needs a friend like you."

"Yeah, maybe." I shrugged, and we moved forward in line.

Ahead of us, in front of the cameras, Lori, Rob, and Mindy hammed it up. Off to the side, Melanie, in her *Bride of Frankenstein* outfit, rolled her made-up eyes. Lori, noticing Melanie, grinned extra wide in her direction. The flashes went off as the photographers captured the moment.

Jackson and I took our turn for pictures and then moved out toward the dance floor. I watched the kids at the punch bowl, the couples doing their best to move to the radio hit the DJ was playing. Then, Melanie and Quinn moseyed out onto the dance floor in their monster costumes. I guessed they would probably be king and queen, the way things went down at this school.

"Hey there, beautiful dame, let's dance," Jackson said, taking hold of my arm gently.

I let him lead me onto the dance floor, wishing that I could just like Jackson back. He was exactly the type of guy I *should* like—the kind who actually cared.

Suddenly, the music changed from the fast pop tune to a romantic ballad. I stood there, not sure what to do. "Awesome transition, DJ," I muttered.

Jackson reached for my hands and pulled me close to dance. "I know you'd rather be listening to something else," he said. "Thanks for pretending."

"Sure," I said. "I'm a good pretender."

He pulled back and studied my face. "Nah. I see through it," he said. "You're not so good with pretending."

I sighed and backed away from him.

"Amy, I'm joking. Come on. Don't walk away. Dance with me."

"'Kay." We started moving again.

"I would never do anything to hurt you," he said almost in a whisper.

"Jackson." I couldn't find the words to tell him I didn't feel any other way about him. I couldn't find the words to tell him that I was confused and mixed up and rejected all in one. It would have been so easy to fall back on Jackson. It felt nice in his arms, but he wasn't for me. And I wasn't going to use him to make me feel better about anything—about myself.

"You're a pretty decent dancer, sailor," I said.

"You're not so bad yourself." Jackson held me tighter.

I tried to squash down the wish that I was with Henry. Henry had been the one person who'd loved me for me. Who, even though it was freaking impossible to be together, had been there for me. And I'd hurt him, obviously. When I told him the truth, he thought it was because I didn't want him. He'd thought I'd wanted him to fade into the future without me—and so he'd sent me away.

He'd been the one rejected, not me. And I'd given up on him so easily. He was the one I wanted to slow dance with. Who I belonged with.

My heart squinched down into a tiny, tiny knot in my chest. And I knew the one place I should be. It wasn't at the dance.

"I still don't get why you wanted to go home so early," Jackson said.

"Thanks. I'll talk to you tomorrow." I gave him a kiss on the cheek and then slammed the truck door shut. I saw Mae's hand pull back the curtain on the living room window, watching our goodbye.

"How was it?" Mae asked as I came into the house.

"A disaster," I said. I slipped off her shoes and got into my boots. "I'll tell you all about it later."

"Amy!" Mae called out, but I was out the back door and down the porch steps.

The rain splashed on my face as I ran through the woodlot. I had to get to Henry. I was suddenly worried that he'd moved forward and that I'd never see him again. I had to make sure he was still out there. I had to find him before it was too late.

Behind me, I could hear Katie barking, but I kept on running. I needed to tell Henry how I felt. Even if Henry's reality was fake, what I'd felt for him had been the real thing. It was clear to me now. And if I couldn't have Henry, at least he had shown me what love looked and felt like.

I shivered with the realization that I loved him. Despite what had happened, despite the fact we could never be together. I loved him. Maybe if he knew that, he would be able to go on and find some kind of happiness. Maybe he'd have the courage to move on and reunite with his brother. Maybe he'd have some faith that his mother was going to be safe. Maybe knowing that what we had shared had been real would set him free.

Yes! My heart soared as the mist came into view, hanging like a shimmering veil in the rainy night. I entered the clearing, feeling it envelop me with its dampness. Tonight it felt delicious, sensuous, on my skin. And maybe that was because it was going to be one of the last times I would feel it. I passed the stump, sprinting the last few yards the best I could in my boots and dress.

Pushing through the barrier to Henry's side sucked the wind out of me, and I stood on the path to the farmhouse, trying to catch my breath. It was still there—everything. The fertile apple tree. The abundant garden. He hadn't moved forward yet. Hadn't moved forward without saying goodbye. That comforted and saddened me all at once.

I took a few steps down the path, noticing the house was illuminated again, white light streaming from all the windows into the night. And there was the stillness again—the uncomfortable stillness that had been there on my last visit. Memories of Henry's anger on the porch flashed through my mind, and I was suddenly struck by the feeling of being unwanted. Of being an intruder.

"You don't belong here," I said aloud. And the words resonated in my bones.

So what if I loved Henry. Did he love me? Mae told me once that love always makes the first move. That love gives without hesitation. But I had been the only one reaching out. I was the one who came into the clearing and found him. I was the one who wanted to cross over to his side. I was the one who had made everything happen.

I stopped on the path, staring toward the house. Maybe Henry would look out the window and see me. Maybe he would come to the clearing and we could be together once more in a place where time didn't exist for either one of us. Thoughts flooded my mind. I was scared of him sending me away. I was scared of him rejecting me again.

And I wanted him to be the one to want me.

I waited on the path, willing him to look out the window. To wonder about me. To come look for me. To risk *something* for me. But he didn't come.

After a few moments, I wandered back down the path into the milky whiteness, not bothering to look back. When I reached the place in the clearing where we'd first met, I unpinned my corsage and placed it on the stump.

"Goodbye," I whispered. "And good luck, Henry."

I walked slowly back through the clearing and broke through on our side. Katie was at the edge of the woodlot, barking like crazy.

"It's okay, girl. I'm right here," I said.

She kept barking ferociously. I ran closer to see what she was going nuts over. And I found Mae unconscious on the ground.

CHAPTER EIGHTEEN

"What are you doing all alone in here?" Grandpa Briggs stood in the doorway.

"Nothing much." Henry sat up on his brother's bed. "Just thinking about Robert," he said.

Grandpa entered and sat down in the desk chair. "I've been doing some thinking, too." Grandpa picked up one of the toy airplanes on Robert's desk and turned the propeller. "You know, son, whatever was going to happen to our family was what was meant to be," he said. "I truly believe the Lord has a plan for all of us."

"This plan wasn't a good one."

"You take the bitter with the sweet," he said. "Can't have one without the other."

"What if it's all bitter?"

"No such thing," Grandpa said with a half smile. He set the airplane back down on the desk. "I've always looked back on the hard times and somehow found the blessings within."

"Well—"

"Henry, something's been bothering me since that night you explained everything to us in the kitchen. You never told us why you prayed that prayer."

"It had to do with Mother," he said.

"I worried it was about her," said Grandpa.

"If we go forward, something bad might happen."

"True. But what if that is what is supposed to happen? And what if something good comes after the bad? If you don't allow the one, then the other doesn't happen, either."

Henry nodded. He looked up at the walls, where Robert had

tacked posters of ships and airplanes. His brother had always been fascinated by the service. He had been ready to go when his turn came up. He had been ready to fight. Henry didn't share his brother's fascination. He never had.

"We can't predict what's going to happen any more than we should command what should happen. That's not for us to say." Grandpa got up from the chair and shuffled to the window. He pulled the curtain back, peering out toward the mist. "Now you have a choice to make."

"I know, sir."

"You let us go forward and let things unfold how they will, or you keep us here in this falsehood."

"But what about Mother? What if she—"

"Then as painful as it would be, son, that is the way it is supposed to be. We live our lives, and then we pass on."

Henry's stomach tensed. "You're saying you don't care if Mother dies."

"I care that your brother *lives*."

"How did you—"

Grandpa turned back toward him. "I found this paper out on the porch swing the last time Amy was here."

Henry reached for the small white square. "She must have left it behind."

"Did you read the date, son? It's in the next *century*, for goodness' sake!"

Henry forced himself to unfold the paper. There it was in black and white. A tiny picture of his brother, old and gray, and there were the dates Grandpa was talking about. "I knew there was something a little peculiar about that girl. Very sweet, but not a bit like us."

"Yes, it's true that she's not from our time. But how do we know she didn't just have this printed up? How do we know this is the truth about Robert?"

"Why would she lie to you? She likes you, and for her to tell you about your brother was the right thing to do. And how did you thank her? By sending her away. And rudely, I might add."

Henry got up from the bed and began to pace the room slowly.

"I think you know what needs to be done," Grandpa said, his voice steely.

"I didn't do this on purpose," Henry said, stuffing his hands in his pockets. "When I prayed that night, I didn't expect a miracle."

"Is it a miracle? Is that what this is? Your mother and I in a fog. The summer stretching into mindlessness. I hardly call that a miracle. In fact, I think the only miracle I have seen around this place lately is Amy." Grandpa gazed sadly at Henry. "If it weren't for that girl, your mother and I wouldn't have woken up to this phony summer. And I dare say that Amy has opened your eyes, too, son."

Henry stopped his pacing. "Yes," he said, quietly, "and if we move forward, then I'll never see her again."

"Ah." Grandpa gave Henry a gentle smile. "There's the rub."

Henry sat back down on the bed. "I've never felt this way about a girl."

"There will be others," Grandpa said.

"No. Not like Amy. I don't want to lose her."

"She knows this is right," Grandpa said. "And the right thing is not always the easiest to do."

After a hard sleep, Henry walked slowly down the sunlit path to the clearing, wishing he'd find Amy waiting for him. She probably hated him for how he'd acted. He had to see her, though. He had to hold her in his arms one more time and tell her goodbye. He couldn't go on without doing that.

The mist felt like a cold, wet shroud as he stepped through it. He shivered and took steps forward. "Amy?" he called, knowing that he had only a pale hope of her being there. No answer from the mist. He walked forward, into the center of the clearing, until he reached the stump. And then he saw the corsage—white gardenias.

Amy had been there, and judging by the freshness of the flowers, it hadn't been that long ago. He called out for her again, but no answer came. And the sobering thought struck him that she'd been there, in the clearing, but she hadn't crossed over to see him.

Suddenly, the flowers in his hand reminded him of a funeral offering, a goodbye without words, without second chances. Amy had left that corsage, never intending to return.

She wasn't coming back.

Tucking the flowers in his pocket, he started walking in the direction of her house. But when he reached the humming edge of the clearing, he hesitated. He hadn't crossed before. He hadn't dared make the jump. He wasn't as brave as Amy. He wasn't ready for everything to collapse—at least not yet.

"Amy?" he called out, one last time. And then, unwilling to cross, he backed slowly into the safety of the mist.

CHAPTER NINETEEN

The beeping of the machines was getting to me. And the smell of bad coffee and ammonia cleaners. And the fact that Mae was lying helpless in the bed.

I shifted in my chair, trying to keep from falling asleep. Through the blinds, I could see thick raindrops splashing down in the hospital parking lot. It was midday, and the TV was running an old cowboy movie, but I'd turned the sound way down. Outside, another ambulance screeched in, sirens blaring.

I touched the pearls around my neck and studied Mae's pale face. Her lips were colorless, her normal smile gone in favor of slackened wrinkles. I pulled the blankets up around her again and reached for her hand. She let out a sigh and rolled her head to the right, but didn't wake up.

"Oh, Amy," my mother said as she and Pete entered the room, shucking their coats. "Why didn't you call us sooner? How is Mae?"

"Not good," I said, glancing over my shoulder and then down at Mae.

Pete came up and gave me an awkward pat on the back since I didn't get up from my chair. "How are you, kiddo?"

"Also not good," I said.

Mom came over and pulled me up from the chair and into a hug. She didn't say anything, but she was breathing deeply, like she was trying to stay calm.

"'Scuse me girls. I'm gonna go find the doc and get up to speed on the situation." Pete left the room, shutting the door softly behind him.

Mom let me go finally and looked down at Mae. "She's lost all her color."

I nodded. "Her heart was really weakened. The surgery was tough on her."

"And you," Mom said, "you look like you've been up all night."

"Yeah, it happened after the dance."

"That explains the dress," she said, gesturing down at my outfit from Friday night.

I shrugged. I hadn't wanted to leave Mae, even for a second, so I hadn't changed when the ambulance arrived. I'd piled in the back with the medics.

"Listen, Ames—I want you to come back home with us. It's clear you can't stay with Mae now."

"She needs me here at the hospital."

Mom smiled gently. "No. I mean permanently. We're almost ready to move down to Phoenix, and it would be best if you come with us."

I bunched Mae's blanket in my fist. "I'm not leaving her."

"A heart bypass is serious stuff," Mom said. "Mae's going to need a lot of help and recuperation time. She's probably going to need to be in a rehabilitation center."

"No way," I said. "I'll help her."

"She'll need nursing—trained care. You can't do that."

"I'll learn. I'm not leaving Mae."

Pete came back into the room. "Doctor said he's been trying to get Mae to take better care of herself for some time. Amy, did you know she was on three different heart medications? Her heart's been weak for years," he said.

I felt a twinge of guilt. "I didn't know she was taking all that medicine," I muttered.

"There was a lot of stress on her heart," Pete continued.

"Yeah, she'd been pushing herself lately. I guess I should have told her to take it easy."

"Well, it's not your fault," Mom said, squeezing my shoulder.

"Yeah, it kind of is," I said. I thought of Mae rushing through the woodlot to find dumb old me wasting my time in the clearing. I had a hand in what had happened to her. I'd spent time chasing after Henry, instead of truly being with Mae. I'd had one foot in the past the whole time I'd been living with her.

"So, in a couple of weeks we'll fly down to the desert," Mom said. "That'll give you time to say your goodbyes."

"Mom, did you not hear me? I'm sorry, but I'm not leaving my town."

"*Your* town? You haven't even been here for two months."

"It's home," I said. "More of a home than I've had in a long time."

Mom blinked at me, and her smile faded. "Do you think that's fair?"

"Mom, it's true. Mae listens to me. And Mae asks me about things. Mae cares."

"I always cared," Mom said.

"It's not the same—and it's not a competition," I said. "I want to stay with Mae. You don't understand."

Mom sighed. "You're being very dramatic. Mae's got a long recovery ahead of her. She can't watch out for you during that."

"No one needs to watch out for me. I'll watch out for her," I said. "I should have been doing that all this time, anyway. I screwed up on that part, I admit."

"Honey, you can't force her to move down with us," Pete offered, putting an arm around my mother.

"True." Mom reached out for my hand. "Look, I don't care how old you are; you're still my little girl. I just want to protect you."

"Seriously?" I felt about ready to explode. She really thought she had any interest in protecting me from anything? That was a change. She hadn't seemed to care about protecting me when

I was with Matt. The words stuck in my throat, but I'm sure my expression said it all.

Mom glanced over at Pete, who was shifting uncomfortably in his chair and then back at me. "Of course I want to protect you. I'm your mother," she said in a quiet voice.

"I think we both know that when I needed your protection, you weren't there," I said, letting out a deep breath.

"Now, that's not fair," Pete said.

"Forget it," I said, shaking my head. "I love you, Mom. But I protect myself now." I turned back to Mae, who was snoring lightly. "And I'm making this decision. I'm sticking with Mae. She needs me as much as I need her."

"Do you think she's going to wake up while I'm gone? I feel bad leaving her tonight," I said, looking over at Jackson hours later. The drive home from the hospital seemed like an endless ride down a long, dark tunnel. I fought to keep my eyes open and resisted the urge to rest my head on Jackson's shoulder.

"Don't feel bad—you're exhausted. She'd want you to rest. I promise I'll pick you up tomorrow and drive you back down. She should be awake by then." Jackson flipped on his truck's windshield wipers.

"Yeah."

"I'll get my sweats back from you then," he said, gesturing to the clothes I'd pulled on at the hospital. "I figured you must have been getting pretty sick of the dress."

"Yeah." I slipped lower in the seat and Jackson turned on the stereo, drowning out the noise of the engine, the noise in my head. It was what I needed more than anything. I wanted to believe that Mae was going to be all right. I wanted to believe I'd be able to take care of her on my own. I wanted to believe that everything—the clearing, Henry—had somehow been worth it, even if it had ended badly, ended with Mae in the shape she was in.

The mournful, melodic guitar chords washed over me, and the darkness of the truck's cab hid my endless supply of tears. I was sure no one, ever, in the whole wide stupid world, felt how I felt in that moment. No one understood me. Not a soul.

We rolled up into the gravel driveway, next to Mae's rig. Jackson turned the stereo way down and slipped the car into Park. Katie trotted around to the passenger side of the truck, waiting.

"Thanks again for coming to get me."

"I'm glad you called," Jackson said. "So, is there anything else I can do? Anything at all that you need? And I'm asking as a friend, Amy."

I wiped my wet cheeks with the sleeve of the borrowed sweatshirt. "No. You did a lot already," I said.

He wrapped me into a sideways hug. "You want me to come in with you, make sure you're gonna be all right?"

"Nah," I said. "I'll get a fire going and feed the dog and we'll be okay." I didn't mention to him how lonely that little trailer was going to feel. How I'd probably cry all night with Katie, missing Mae.

Jackson let go of me, looking as if he felt helpless. But I knew there was nothing he could do or say to make anything better.

"Thanks," I said.

He gave me a soft smile. "You get some sleep tonight and I'll come get you after lunch, around one. That cool?"

"Yeah, that'd be great. Really, I appreciate it. You're a good guy," I said.

"Thanks. You are, too," he said. "A good person, I mean, not a guy."

"I know what you mean," I said, grabbing my plastic bag of

clothes from the floor. I let myself out and waved at Jackson from the porch. Once Katie and I were inside the house, through the windows I watched him slowly back down the drive.

It was chilly in the trailer, and the sound of the rain beating down on the metal roof made it feel even colder. I got kindling arranged, along with some paper shreds, and started the fire as Mae had shown me. In just a little while I had a small blaze started. I added some sticks to the pile and clanked the stove door shut. Over at the rack by the door, I slipped off my heavy coat and stuck it on a hook.

And then in the pile of shoes underneath, I saw Mae's rubber boots—standing vacantly.

I held back a sob. "She's going to be okay," I said aloud. "She's going to be freaking okay!" I was shivering, so I grabbed my coat back off the hook and wrapped it around my shoulders. I had to get this place warm.

Katie joined me over at the wood stove, watching me snap more small sticks and set them atop the burning pile. She nosed my hand until I pet her, and then I was crying again, hugging her and burying my face in her fur.

"She's fine, Katie-dog," I said, trying to calm myself down again.

And then lights hit the front windows as someone started up our driveway. Jackson had come back! I don't think I'd ever been more glad that he showed so much interest in me. He must have been able to tell that I didn't want to be alone.

I so wanted someone else—someone besides myself—to tell me everything was going to be all right. And in that moment, I didn't care if it was true or not, I just needed to hear the words.

Anxiously, I shut the wood stove door, wiped my face with my coat sleeve again, and went to answer the door. "Jackson, I'm so—"

I heard, "Hey, babe."

And Matt Parker stepped into the lighted doorway.

CHAPTER TWENTY

This was going to be it. Henry knelt down beside his bed, as he had so many nights before, and clasped his hands together. But tonight would be different. Tonight he would undo, if he could, what he had done. And tomorrow life would go on as it should have. He supposed it was the right thing to do now, but that didn't make it easier.

"Henry?"

He looked up to see his mother standing in her blue night-gown in the doorway. Her eyes were clear and open, her smile tentative, as if she expected him to shoo her away.

"Yes, Mother?" he said. "Can I get you something?"

"I don't mean to disturb you. You go on ahead and say your prayers. I'll see you in the morning." She came in and bent down to kiss him on the cheek. "Don't worry. I'm not afraid," she whispered in his ear as she pulled away.

Henry reached out for her hand. "What do you mean?"

His mother sat down on the bed. "Grandpa told me your fears for me, but I'm not afraid. We all have paths to walk. If I wake up tomorrow and don't remember any of this, and if something bad happens, it was meant to happen. I'm not afraid of that, and I hope you won't be, either."

"I can't let you hurt yourself," Henry said, his jaw clenching. The words felt odd to say aloud.

Mother smiled tenderly. "I haven't been well. I'm sorry you had to endure that along with me. It's a terrible thing to want to give up on life, to feel there is no way out."

Henry said, "It's not your fault. You've had an extra helping of sorrow."

"I'm trying to do better, son. And somehow, through all of this, I think you've helped me." She patted her pocket where she normally kept her pills. "Empty," she said. "That day I got lost, I sat near the creek and thought about taking down the whole bottle. But the pills make me fuzzy, and I didn't want to be fuzzy anymore. I'd been fuzzy all this long summer. I'm ready to live, to see what happens. Aren't you?"

Henry nodded slowly. "Yes, ma'am."

"Look, son, sometimes you have to trust that everything's going to turn out the way it should. That's part of living—and love, too." Her eyes were shining in the lamplight, and she had the softest of smiles on her face.

"Trust," he repeated.

"You have to trust that all of this has been for a reason. That's what I feel. Don't you feel that it has, too?"

Henry's throat tightened so he couldn't speak. He got up from the floor and embraced his mother.

"Amy is here for a reason," she said. "Don't worry about what happens tomorrow. Worry about what's happening in your heart. Go and tell her how you feel before it's too late."

"And what if I can't come back?" he said, vocalizing the darkest fear he held. "What if everything disappears and I'm lost—we're all lost—forever?"

"Then that was meant to be as well," she said.

Henry strode through the mist, fortifying his confidence with deep breaths. When he reached the edge—Amy's side—he hesitated at the sound of humming, the electric buzz that marked the boundary. It was going to hurt. Then, reminding himself that this was the only way to reach Amy, he plunged through the last barrier.

He stumbled out into a large meadow of overgrown grass. The transition had knocked the wind out of him, and for a moment, he sucked in air like a drowning man. His first thought was to look down at himself. He'd just traveled forward more years than he cared to think about, but his hands were smooth, and as he ran his fingertips over his face, his skin felt unwrinkled, still young. Relieved, he continued on through the field, rain soaking his clothes and hair. He would be a mess when he found Amy, but he didn't care about that. And he knew she wouldn't, either. He couldn't wait to hold her in his arms.

Ahead was a woodlot. He hurried down its well-worn path toward lights. He passed several cords of meticulously stacked firewood and came upon a flat-roofed house, like train cars put together. A German shepherd ran around the corner toward Henry, barking madly.

"Easy," he said, holding out a hand.

The dog slowed, and then whining, came up to sniff Henry. She was friendly; that was good. The shepherd followed him as he stepped up the back porch to a large glass window that looked into a parlor. His breath caught in his chest.

Inside, Amy was sitting on a sofa with a dark-haired boy. They were talking—the boy wearing a smug expression, and Amy looking tense. Henry watched them sitting there, alarm and confusion pulsing through him.

After a moment, Amy saw Henry through the glass. She opened the back door and came out onto the porch. Her eyes appeared tired, with dark makeup ringing them, as if she'd been crying. "What are you doing here?" she demanded.

"I—I . . ." Henry's voice didn't seem to work. He stood there, dripping rain, and staring at Amy, all hope of a happy welcome dissolving.

"You crossed over?"

"I had to."

For a second, Amy's expression changed, softened into the sweet, understanding smile he had expected. But then concern took over her face again. "You have to go."

Henry's heart constricted. Something was definitely wrong. He surveyed Amy's strange outfit—some kind of gymnasium sweater and pants, and a beautiful string of pearls around her neck. It didn't make sense, even for Amy's sense of future style.

"You left the flowers for me," he said, unable to keep his gaze from wandering to the boy on the couch. "I thought that you—"

"I'm glad you came to see me, but now's not a good time," Amy said. She reached a hand out and touched Henry on the chest. "We'll just talk later, okay?"

"Okay, so who's this dude?" Issuing an irritated grunt, the boy who'd been on the couch pushed past Amy in the open doorway. He stood behind Amy, placing a hand on her shoulder. "Some country bumpkin giving you trouble?"

Henry planted his feet and looked the boy square in the eyes. "I'm Henry Briggs."

"Yay for you," the boy said. "Come on, babe. Shut the door and let me warm you up." He ran a hand down Amy's arm.

"What's the big idea?" Henry's voice was sharp.

"I want to talk to you, but later, okay? Matt showed up and—"

"Matt Parker?" Henry's blood rushed to his ears. At his sides, his hands balled into fists. "This is the creep you mentioned."

Amy moved closer to Henry and said, "It's fine. I've got it handled."

"Who're you calling a creep?" Matt took a step toward Henry, his lip curling.

"Anyone who'd treat a lovely girl like Amy the way you have is a creep in my book," Henry said. "You're a disgrace. I oughta sock you."

"Sock me? I haven't heard that one in a while." Matt laughed and pushed Amy out of the way, stepping onto the back porch. The German shepherd whined at Amy's side.

"Okay, stop. That's enough." Amy tugged on Matt's jacket sleeve, but he didn't seem to care.

Henry stood chest to chest with the boy who'd broken Amy's spirit and her heart. He wanted to pound him into a bloody mess. "Someone ought to teach you a lesson," he said, leveling his gaze at the creep.

"And that someone's you, farmer?" Matt said.

"Knock it off!" Amy pushed the two boys apart and stood between them. "Just freaking back off, both of you!"

"No, I want to see what farmer thinks he's bringing," Matt said.

"I'll be bringing you a shiner," Henry said.

Amy grabbed Henry's hand and pulled him away from Matt, into a shadowy corner of the deck. "I've got this. It's not what you think, okay?"

"What *should* I think? You told me you were through with the likes of him. Don't you understand that you deserve so much more?"

"I do understand that, Henry. Trust me!" Amy's eyes flashed with anger. She let go of Henry's hand. "You need to leave now."

Henry felt a coldness that sank into his bones. "I can't let you return to him."

"Just go!" Amy stared him down, until Henry backed away from her and down the steps.

If she really wanted him to go, then well, that was that. No sad goodbye. No kiss for him to hold in his memory for the days to come. Nothing. Not what he expected, and not enough. She'd chosen someone who'd used her and thrown her away. She'd chosen that creep over him. He couldn't understand it. The pain of rejection seared through him. Somehow maybe that would make it easier to never see Amy ever again, but he didn't want to let it end like this. He couldn't.

Matt Parker, wearing a smile of triumph, gave Henry a finger wave. "So long, farmer."

Henry continued to back away down the path. Amy stared out at him defiantly, but behind the defiance, Henry saw fear. She wasn't all right. She didn't want him to go. And he wasn't about to, anyway.

He took a deep breath and slid into the trees where he could keep watch.

CHAPTER TWENTY-ONE

Sending Henry away was the hardest thing ever, but I knew I had to do this on my own. Matt was *my* problem. I'd called him the other night. In my desperation, I'd somehow summoned him here by reaching out. But maybe it was good to be face-to-face with him. There were things I wanted to say, things we needed to talk about, things Henry didn't need to hear.

"Come on," I said, turning to Matt. He followed me into the house and plopped back down on the couch. I stayed on my feet, watching him relax into the pillows.

"That guy was a tool," Matt said, with a smug laugh.

I decided not to comment. Wrapping my arms across my stomach, I took a seat on the couch corner Matt wasn't occupying. Katie settled on her bed near the wood stove, her brown eyes watching us, her ears up, listening.

"So, you were about to tell me how you found this place?"

"I asked at the gas station about your aunt Mae," Matt said. "Everyone knows her. She went into the hospital, huh?"

"Yeah."

"Cool, so the house is ours, right?"

"Uh . . . what? My aunt's had a heart attack—she's really sick. It's not like I'm hosting a house party here," I said.

"On the phone the other night, when you called me, it sounded like you couldn't wait to see me. So, here I am. You sounded like you really missed me, babe."

"I did miss you, it's just—"

"What? Farmer guy? Please. That's hilarious."

"Look, why did you come here? Was it just to put me down or what?"

"Whoa—attitude," Matt said. "I just want to take your mind off things for a while."

I totally knew what he was talking about, so I rolled my eyes. "You really came all this way for that."

"For you." His face softened and his smile seemed genuine. He swung his feet off the couch onto the floor and scooted down next to me. "I love you, babe." The words that once meant so much to me coming from him sounded flat.

"Love?" I said. "You really think this is—*was*—love?"

"Yeah." He leaned back into the couch cushion, appraising me. "You said you loved me, too. Remember that?" he said in a soft voice, his blue eyes lowered.

"Matt, I'm pretty sure that wasn't love," I said.

"Well, aren't you Miss High and Mighty now," he said, rebounding with a laugh. "Farmer boy teach you about love, Amy? What—does he have a sexy tractor?"

I hugged a throw pillow to my chest. Now that I had Matt in front of me, I needed to focus on what I wanted to say. "This is about you and me—not him."

"Is it? Because the old Amy would be over here making out with me right now," he said, reaching his hand out to me. "What happened to you?"

"What happened to *me*? What happened to *you*?" I got up from the couch and tossed the pillow into the nearest chair. "What happened to the nice guy who took me to the movies and wrote me sweet notes in class?"

"Hey, I would still do that kind of stuff."

"No—I mean *what happened* to that guy? 'Cause he got replaced with someone who pushed me into walls, who threw beer cups at me, who slapped me."

"What are you talking about?"

My stomach tightened. "We both know exactly what I'm talking about."

Matt's face reddened, and then, after a moment of staring me down, he said, "Why do you have to bring up old stuff? How many times can a guy apologize for all that?"

"Never enough times," I said, pushing back the tears inside that were threatening to ruin everything. "'Cause I told you to stop, but you kept doing it. And doing it."

Matt got up from the couch and moved toward me. Instinctively I held my hands out.

He let out a dry-sounding laugh. "Seriously? C'mon—I'm just gonna hug you," he said.

"Don't touch me, Matt. I don't want you to hug me. Just sit down, okay?"

"Oh, you gonna tell me what to do now?" he said, raising his voice.

"No, I'm asking you to calm down. Please."

He took another step toward me. "You're the one who needs to calm down."

"I am calm. I'm calm and I'm telling you what you did was wrong. How you treated me was wrong. The things you—"

"Yeah?" Matt was in my face now. "You really think that? Is that the reason you left school like a little baby? Came out here to live in this crappy trailer in this stupid town? If I was the one in the wrong, why did *you* leave?"

That stung like a slap. I took a deep breath. "You know what you did—what you do—is wrong." I held my stance, even though Matt was up close to me. Katie growled from her dog bed.

Matt reached out toward me and I flinched. "Really? You think I'd hurt you? I love you," he said. "Why you gotta be like that?"

"You need to go," I said, nearly shaking as I stood there now. "Just please go."

"So it's like that?"

"Yeah."

He got up close in my face again and it scared me. But the difference between before and now was that I wasn't going to accept it; I wasn't going to make excuses for him; I wasn't going to let him get away with anything anymore.

He reached toward my hair like he was going to grab my head. Growling deeply, Katie slowly moved toward us, baring her teeth.

"Easy, there, dumb mutt." He held his hands up and moved back from me. "See, I'm leaving now." He glanced from Katie to me. "You sure you want me to go? Once I leave, I'm never coming back."

"Perfect," I said.

Matt threw open the door and marched out onto the porch. I followed him. Rain was streaming down, but neither one of us was paying any attention to that.

"This is your last chance," he said. "I know it could be better between us. I know I could treat you right if you let me."

"I'm gonna treat *myself* right. I don't need you to do that for me."

He glared, then stomped down the porch steps, followed closely by Katie. I watched as he climbed into his truck and slammed the door. And then he tore off down the driveway, leaving only a ripple on the mud puddles where his rig had been.

Gone. He was gone.

The rain mixed with my tears. I buckled over onto the porch, crying for me then and me now. Crying it all out. Crying it all away.

And then arms were around me. Wet, warm arms were pulling me up to my feet and holding me. "I'm here," Henry said, rocking me against the rain. "I'm here, sweetheart."

"I told you to leave." I sobbed into his already-wet shirt.

"I wasn't about to leave you alone with him."

"I had to tell him," I said, sucking in my breath. "I had to tell him on my own."

Henry kissed my forehead. "You did so well." He stroked my hair and held me tighter. "Everything's going to be all right."

And I felt so strong. And I felt so loved.

CHAPTER TWENTY-TWO

"It's not much, but . . ."

"It's fine." Henry glanced around the trailer. It was cozy enough, and it was dry. He hadn't expected anything grandiose.

"Be right back," Amy said.

Henry tried to contain his dripping to the few squares of tiling near the wood stove and couldn't help but gawk at the contents of the room. A big, rounded sofa was positioned under the front windows, and a wood cabinet at the end of the room held several things that looked electric. Little lights decorated their black fronts, including a bright green 12:00 that flashed repeatedly. Beneath those machines, he saw his reflection in the glass screen of what had to be a television. He'd only read about those in science magazines; he didn't know anyone who'd seen one in real life.

Shaking his head, he gave the German shepherd another pat and then added sticks to the fire. Soon he had the blaze stoked up and crackling away.

Amy returned in pajamas a moment later, carrying a stack of towels.

"Thank you. I haven't felt a good rain since I don't know when," Henry said, taking the towel Amy held out to him. "Mighty refreshing," he said with a nervous laugh.

Amy stood by the couch, watching him. "You're soaked. Do you want a bathrobe or something?"

"That'd be swell." A minute later, Henry was returning from the bathroom, dressed in the thick, white robe, which smelled of

Amy's flowery soap, and hanging up his wet clothes near the wood stove to dry. The fire was warming up the room at last, and Amy had fixed them both mugs of tea. The lights were low, and it was about as cozy as Henry could have imagined the future to be.

"Better?" Amy asked.

"Yes," he said, taking a seat beside her on the sofa.

"It's been a terrible evening," she said.

"Yes, I know."

"No, it's not just Matt. My aunt's really ill. I'm so scared." Amy leaned her head on him, and he wrapped an arm around her thin shoulders.

"I'm with you now. Don't worry," he said, kissing the top of her head.

"How did you know Matt was here?" Amy picked up her mug and took a sip.

"I didn't. I came here tonight for something else," Henry said. "I'm so sorry about the other night. You were right to tell me about Robert. You were right about everything. I need to go on. I need to see what happens."

Amy set her tea down. "So, this is it? You're moving on?"

He nodded. "I couldn't leave without seeing you. Without telling you . . ."

"Without telling me what?"

"I think you know." He held her chin up and planted the lightest kiss on her lips. When he pulled back, Amy's eyes were closed, her long eyelashes still rain logged, makeup smeared around them—but so beautiful.

"Tell me, Henry. Tell me and mean it." It was a demand and a prayer all in one.

"I love you," he said, kissing the bridge of her nose. "I've loved you since I met you. And I'll love you forever." He gazed into Amy's brown eyes, wanting her to know everything that was inside him, everything that he'd been holding at a distance. "I know you can't come with me, but I'll take you wherever I go. I'll remember you always."

Tears trailed down Amy's cheeks. "Me, too," she said. And she threw her arms around him, burying her face in his chest.

He kissed the top of her damp head. "Tell me, Amy. Tell me and mean it," he whispered.

"I love you, Henry Briggs," she said. "And I mean it."

He had to kiss her then. And Amy kissed him back. And the kiss deepened into more than a kiss. Henry pulled Amy on top of him, and for the moment there were only the two of them and the kiss taking a shape of its own.

A kiss that would have to last him a lifetime.

Minutes later, Henry was nearly trembling as Amy led him to her bedroom. "Stay with me for a little while longer," she said.

"Are you sure about this?"

"I want to fall sleep with you holding me," Amy said. "I promise I'll be a perfect gentlewoman."

And Henry knew he didn't want her to be that way. He wanted her to need him as badly as he did her. But he climbed into the clean, crisp sheets next to Amy and let her cuddle up next to him. Her hair was dry now and held that maddening smell of flowers. He tried not to think about her in her thin pajamas, of the feel of her shape curled against him.

"Hold me tighter," Amy said, her lips moving closer to his neck, so that he could almost feel them on his skin. "I want to remember this." There was pain in her voice, a pain Henry recognized.

"Don't think about tomorrow," he said.

"How can I not?"

He found her lips in the dark and kissed her again. And then she was kissing him back and crying at the same time.

"None of that," Henry said, kissing her chin, then her nose, then her cheeks and forehead.

"Henry . . . would you, um, do you want to . . ." Amy had stopped crying, and her voice was soft across the pillows.

At first he didn't know what to say. Of course he wanted Amy, wanted her more than anything. "We don't have to . . ." he said. "I'm not expecting anything."

"I want to. I want to pretend my first time was with you," Amy said.

And Henry closed his eyes and for the first time in his endless summer, let everything just happen as it would.

CHAPTER TWENTY-THREE

I woke up and found Henry sitting on the edge of my bed. He was framed in shadows, but I could see he'd put on his dried clothes and abandoned my robe on the hamper in the corner. I thought about how safe I'd felt with Henry, how comfortable it had been with his arms around me. How different it had been from what I'd experienced with Matt. Henry had been right—when you truly loved someone, it made everything better.

"What's going on?" I said, moving up onto my elbows.

He smiled. "Just watching you sleep."

I glanced toward the windows. It was dark, but I didn't hear rain pounding on the roof anymore. I was sleepy, and all I wanted was for Henry to climb back into the sheets with me. "What time is it?"

"It's late."

A silence fell between us. It wasn't only late outside; it was late for Henry. I knew what was coming next. "I don't want you to go," I said.

Henry nodded. "I don't want to, either, but it's the only way this ends."

I gathered the sheets and blankets in my fists, pulling them up around me. I tried to take deep breaths, but only shallow ones came and I started to feel dizzy. Henry reached for my hands, forcing them to relax as he pulled me up to a sitting position.

"You need to be strong," he said. "And from what I saw earlier tonight, that comes easy for you."

"What, are you just going to walk out the door and be gone

forever? You're just going to leave me here in the dark?"

"Amy, don't."

"I'm going with you. I'm going with you into the mist." I scrambled out of bed and rummaged in the closet for clothes, throwing on jeans and a sweatshirt.

Henry sat on the bed, watching me. "Amy," he whispered, his voice breaking, "this is hard for me, too."

I stopped in the midst of looking for socks and sneakers.

"You know you can't go, any more than I can stay." He moved to the window and stared out at the back field, at the stretch of trees before the mist. When he turned back to me, his voice was low. "I love you. I meant it when I said it before, and I mean it now. Nothing that happened between us tonight changes that. The distance and time between us doesn't change it. The fact that we can't be together doesn't change it, either."

I dropped the shoe in my hand and went to hug him at the window. "I love you, too."

"Then walk me to the clearing one last time."

The path through the woodlot had never seemed so short. Every step I took brought me closer to losing Henry forever. And every step seemed to make me angrier. It wasn't fair that now that I'd finally learned what true love was, it was going to disappear. But maybe that's the price of love—that you don't know how long it's going to last. And you don't know how bad it's going to hurt when it goes away.

"What's the plan?" I asked.

Henry paused to pat Katie-dog where we stood at the edge of the mist. "I'm going to change my prayer tonight, and if it works, then the rest of my life begins."

"And Robert will come home," I said.

"Hopefully, Mother will be around to see that. I don't know what's going to happen. To me, to any of us."

"You're going to do great things."

"I don't know about that," Henry said.

"No, that was a very important time in our history," I said. "I just mean that whatever you and Robert end up doing in the war, you're making a big difference."

A flicker of fear shone in Henry's eyes. "Is it—"

"Yeah, it's almost over, Henry." I reached for his hand.

"Thank you, Amy," he said. "I wouldn't be at this crossroads if you hadn't come along."

I shrugged. "Maybe."

"No maybes." Henry kissed me on the cheek. "Thank you for showing me how life could be."

I started crying then, because it all felt so final. Henry wrapped his arms around me and squeezed me tight. I inhaled the scent of his skin and soap and touched his sandy blond hair, willing my fingers to remember the way it felt. I didn't want to forget any of this. I didn't want this moment to end.

Henry kissed my lips softly and then pulled back to look at me. "Amy, you deserve so much more than you've been given. I know you'll find someone, someday, who's worthy of your love. Don't settle for anything less. Promise me."

I nodded because I couldn't speak. I couldn't tell him that I didn't want to believe what he was saying, that I'd never love anyone the way I loved him. I couldn't tell him my heart was breaking in so many more ways than I ever knew it could.

Henry's eyes welled with tears he refused to acknowledge. He reached out one more time to smooth my hair away from my eyes. "Goodbye, love."

And then he let me go and walked into the mist alone.

After he faded away into the clearing, I walked back to Mae's. I pulled off my clothes and got into bed. Sobbing, I scrunched the covers over my head. I breathed in the faint smell of Henry's soap still left on the pillows. I listened to the rain starting up again and Katie snoring at my side.

And I wished myself far, far away. Only I stayed there in my bed missing him. And then at last, mercifully, the dark took me.

CHAPTER TWENTY-FOUR

I blink awake to sunlight. A big German shepherd is sleeping at the foot of my bed. I sit up because I hear someone whistling a happy tune. And then my door opens and a graying old woman stands there smiling at me.

"Amy, sweetie! Up and at 'em! Uncle Joe's making pancakes."

"Great-Aunt Mae?"

"Well, who else would it be? Let's go!"

The dog follows Mae out of the room. I look around, but everything seems strange. There's an oak dresser and a desk with a shiny laptop on it. The curtains are a cheerful yellow, and the room is large and bright. I slip out of the bed and go to the window. I'm on the second story and from here I can see a garden of winter vegetables, and a large apple tree that's lost its leaves. The view seems familiar, yet alien.

I realize I'm in underwear, so I open the closet and take out a white robe. Tying the belt, I walk out into the hallway. Pictures line the walls. I recognize Aunt Mae, along with a man who must be Uncle Joe. Military pictures of the man in uniform. There are my baby pictures. Pictures of me and my mom. Pictures of me with a familiar-looking boy my age. I sit down on the step, feeling strange and trying to figure out why things seem so fuzzy.

"You all right, sweetie?" Mae says, following me down the stairs.

"Mae, where'd all the pictures come from?"

She laughs. "They've only been here every summer you've spent up here in the valley with us! And that's been since you were, what, eleven?"

"Who's this?" I say, pointing at the picture of me with a mystery boy.

"Oh, I get it—this is some kind of a senility test? Fine, I'll play," she says. "That, my dear, is your first and only boyfriend, Jackson. You've been spending time with him each summer since you were thirteen. Such a nice boy."

"Who's this?" I point at the pictures of her with the man.

"Uncle Joe."

"And here?" I say, pointing at a military photo.

"That's your uncle when he was in the Marines during the war. That boy there next to him, Henry Briggs, saved Joe at Iwo Jima."

My skin pricks with goose bumps, but I'm not sure why. "Briggs?"

Mae nods. "Henry befriended Joe from the first minute he met him. Seemed to always be watching over my Joe. Good man. After the war, Henry's brother, Robert, ended up selling this house to my daddy. Robert and his family moved into town."

"This house?"

"We almost lost it in a kitchen fire years ago, but Joe was able to extinguish the flames."

I have to ask, and I'm not sure why, "What happened to Henry?"

"Missing in action. Never came back from the war. His family was quite sad, especially his mother. But they were also proud that Henry saved my Joe."

"Your Joe?"

Mae taps a wedding photograph farther down the wall. "Married forever now," she says with a giggle. "Come on—did I pass the test? Yes? Then let's go eat some breakfast."

We go down the stairs, passing through a formal parlor with a piano, and enter a sunlit kitchen. An old guy places a stack of pancakes in front of us.

"Now, easy on the butter, my darling Mae," he says, sliding the dish toward me instead. "You've gotta watch the old ticker."

Mae beams at him. "You always take such good care of me."

"My pleasure," Joe says, bending down to kiss her on the cheek. "Eat up now, girls, and then we'll head down to the creek to toss out a few flies."

I eat a pancake, but my stomach is flip-floppy. I down the last of my juice and put my dirty plate in the sink, and then I follow the old couple out to the porch.

"Will you look at that," Joe says, tipping his hat toward the backyard. "Never seen anything like it."

I turn to see what he's talking about. It's some drifting mist settling over the back field. It's mesmerizing. I can't help staring at it.

Moments later while Joe and Mae round up the fly-fishing tackle, I wander toward the mist. I can't explain why, but I feel pulled toward the coolness of the white fog filling the clearing behind the farmhouse.

As I draw closer, everything starts to feel more familiar. My heart feels full. And I sense, somehow, that this morning is full of possibilities.

ACKNOWLEDGMENTS

Thank you to my dedicated literary agent, Stephen Barbara, and to my enthusiastic editor, Julie Tibbott, and her wonderful team at HMH, who believed in *The Clearing* from the start.

A frosting-covered thank-you goes to my friend Julie Blattberg, who listened to my ramblings of the book's concept over chocolate layer cake and encouraged me to bring the project to life. Thanks also to my writing mentor and friend, Pat White, and to Dona Sarkar and the Buzz Girls, my teen fiction blog sisters at BooksBoysBuzz.com, for their unflagging support.

I am also very indebted to Gordon Rottman, World War II guru and writer, for his help with dates and protocol, and to my friends and family who shared their stories and remembrances of the 1940s. I am humbled by your tales of sacrifice and service.

And above all, special thanks to my father, John-Carl Davis, who used to sing "Time in a Bottle" to me every night when I was a little girl. The inspiration has lasted a lifetime.

HEATHER DAVIS spent seven years living in the Upper Skagit Valley of Washington, where *The Clearing* takes place. Like her protagonist, Amy, she had to get used to rural life in the valley—learning farm chores and absorbing the culture of the small town, which was quite different from where she grew up in urban Seattle. The beauty of the valley and her fascination with the "Greatest Generation"—those Americans who lived through World War II—inspired Heather to write this story. She is also the author of *Never Cry Werewolf*.

www.heatherdavisbooks.com